WANTED

DELIGHT BOOK ONE

JENNAE VALE

CHAPTER 1

THE CAIRNGORMS, SCOTLAND - JANUARY
1747

*B*reathing was becoming harder and harder the further up Ben Macdhui Mountain they climbed. Bearnard Fletcher led his brothers Kade and Payton higher than they'd ever been in their lives.

"Bear, can we no' stop?" Kade asked, gasping for breath and looking for all the world as though he might collapse at any moment. "We've been at this for hours. I don't think I can go on much longer." Weak from hunger and with a bleeding head wound, Kade was struggling to keep up.

"If we stop now, we'll be caught. 'Tis no' much farther, lads," Bear assured himself as much as his brothers. He glanced back to see Payton was stoically making the climb. He hadn't uttered a word since their narrow escape. "Payton?"

His brother glanced up at him.

Bear was worried for him. Payton had lost much more than his home and now here they were close to starving to death as they did their best to outrun the English. "Are ye well?"

Payton only nodded and continued climbing.

"Help me with Kade." Bear wrapped an arm around his brother's waist and placed Kade's arm around his neck. Payton did the same on the other side. The brothers carefully made their way upwards, slipping on icy patches and clawing their way over the rocks as they searched for hand and footholds.

"There's a cave not far now. I can see it. We'll shelter there." Bear's fingers latched onto a nearby outcropping to pull himself up. His hands ached from the cold. It was his duty to see that his brothers survived, because it had been his idea to reave a cow from the Sassenachs who'd confiscated all of theirs.

Life hadn't been easy since Culloden. The dragoons had been hunting down the survivors all across the Highlands. If he and his brothers were caught, they'd hang. If they were lucky, they'd avoid the noose and find themselves shipped off to the colonies as slaves. Bear didn't care for either of those options. He wanted his land back, his life back, he wanted things to be the way they once were. The family farm had been taken away along with all their belongings and food. And yet, how could he complain? The same had happened to all his neighbors. They, too, had lost everything. Left with nothing, they'd moved on, scattering across the Highlands. Some moving to Edinburgh and others to seek employment with those English sympathizers who managed to maintain their homes and lands. The difference for Bear was that he wasn't content to allow it. He couldn't stand idly by and see the world he'd once known decimated by those who thought the people of the Highlands inferior.

He climbed up the final few feet using every ounce of energy left in his body, unsure he'd make it. Once there he lay on his back sucking the thin, cold air into his aching lungs, but only for a moment. He then reached down and pulled as Payton shoved Kade up onto the ledge and then joined his brothers as they stared up at the white, cloud-filled sky.

"Is it going to snow?" Kade asked, glancing wearily up at the sky.

"It seems we've made it just in time," Bear answered as the first flakes of snow settled on their upturned faces. "Come. The cave's right here." He stood, holding his hand out for Kade to take. Bear noted the pale color of his brother's skin, the weakness in his grasp, and wondered if he'd survive this ordeal. He'd wanted to leave Kade behind in their makeshift camp, but he'd insisted on joining his brothers. Now, here he was injured, hungry and exhausted. Bear regretted giving in to him. Why had he dragged them all off on this fool's errand? He should have known they'd be seen.

Quiet as mice they'd snuck into the field that held *their* cattle. They made it into the middle of the herd, tying a rope around the neck of one cow and wishing they could take them all. As they began their trek back the way they'd come, the alarm was sounded and they'd left their prize behind, running as fast as they could into the surrounding woods. They'd run and run until Kade tripped and fell face first to the ground, smashing his head on a jagged rock. Bear could hear the sounds of the dragoons crashing through the trees and brush. They had to keep going, but he wouldn't leave his brother behind. Payton helped him lift Kade, dazed and barely conscious, then they found some bramble bushes to hide among as the dragoons scoured the area and continued on. They had stayed that way for hours and when the morning light began to peek down through the trees, they'd moved on, heading to the only place Bear felt there would be safety.

The interior of the cave was cold, but it did offer shelter from the falling snow and the winds that had begun howling.

"Bear, what of *Am Fear Liath Mr*?" Kade asked.

"The Grey Man?" Bear asked.

"Aye. He lives here, ye ken."

"'Tis only a myth, Kade," Payton spoke for the first time and Bear was relieved to hear his voice.

"I believe it. Do ye no' feel his presence?" Kade glanced nervously around the cave, which stretched far back into the mountain. He winced as he turned back and Bear noted that Kade held his head and blinked a few times, his eyes seeming unable to focus.

"Nae," Payton answered. "How long do ye think we should stay here? I fear we'll be snowed in if this storm continues."

"Yer right. We'll stay 'til we get our strength back and then we'll be on our way." Bear slid down the wall of the cave to sit on the cold ground painfully aware of how ill prepared they were. They had no food, nothing to make a fire and only the clothes on their backs. The barren, treeless land of the mountain top was inhospitable at best, leaving little for them to survive on and only this cave for shelter. The only good thing about it was that the English would never believe that this was where they would choose to hide.

Kade and Payton sat beside Bear as they huddled together shivering and miserable.

"Let me take a look at yer head," Bear said, reaching for the scrap of kilt wrapped around his head.

"'Tis fine," Kade answered, batting Bear's hand away.

"I should change yer bandage."

"Leave me be. 'Tis yer only kilt. Ye can no' afford to lose anymore of it."

Bear didn't argue with him. If need be, he'd have Payton hold him down while he tended to his wound, but for now, he'd do as Kade asked and leave him be. He would keep an eye on him. His head wound was concerning, but as with everything of late, there was nothing he could do about it. Anger filled him. Anger at himself. Anger at the English. He pulled in a deep breath, gritting his teeth to keep himself from screaming in frustration.

Kade stirred next to him. "Where will we go?" he asked through chattering teeth.

"We can no' go home," Payton replied in a voice tinged by bitterness. "Those bastards have taken everything from us."

Payton had lost more than his brothers. He'd lost his wife and bairn to a fever that swept through their clan. Weak from a lack of food and exposure to the elements after their home had been burned to the ground by the English, there was little Payton could do to save them. The brothers were without a place to live, but that was easier to remedy. There was no replacement for Payton's loss.

"We'll find a place to call home." Bear wanted to sound sure of himself. For his brothers' sake he hoped he did. "For now, rest." He closed his eyes and thought of a warm fire, a dram of whisky and four walls protecting them.

❄

Upon awakening, Bear was overcome with an uneasy feeling. They weren't alone. He couldn't see anyone in the total darkness of the cave but there was a presence. They must have slept well into the night. He quickly checked Kade to be sure he was still breathing and was relieved he was. Looking out of the mouth of the cave, he knew they were in trouble. Morning would be breaking soon and the mouth of the cave was filling with snow. If they were going to get out, it had to be now.

"Payton, Kade!" he shouted, scaring them both awake. "We must leave." Bear stood and headed to the cave opening. He started clearing the way shoving piles of snow to the side so they could escape. Peering out all he could see was white and a faint glow of light on the horizon. "I fear if we wait any longer we'll be here until spring."

"Will we make it?" Kade asked, glancing behind himself into the darkness of the cave.

"We have to." Bear said.

The three men stepped out onto the ledge just as a loud howling sound came from within the cave and a thunderous roar came from above them.

"Run," Bear shouted.

They didn't get far before they were caught by a wall of snow making its way down the mountain. Tumbling into darkness, Bear's only thought was for Kade and Payton.

The Sierra Nevada, California Present Day

"The slopes on Hill Six are clear." Kirsten Hunter placed the binoculars she'd been peering through onto the window ledge of the lookout tower where she watched and waited. The storm last night had dropped several feet of snow in a matter of hours. Conditions were perfect for an avalanche and the local ski resort thought it best to start a controlled snowslide before skiers would be able to safely head down the slopes.

"I'll radio the artillery operator," said Tim Murray, her partner in crime for the day.

Kirsten placed the binoculars to her eyes once again. "Is it weird that I find this exciting?" she asked.

"No. Not at all. As long as no one gets hurt, it's kind of exciting to see." Tim joined her at the window, perhaps standing a bit too close for Kirsten's comfort.

They'd dated a few times over the past month and Kirsten knew right away that there wasn't anything there for her. Tim, on the other hand, had a totally different take. She didn't have the heart to hurt his feelings, so Kirsten kept going along with his plans. She inched away on the pretense of getting a better view.

The first blast of artillery fire hit the slope they were observing and the snow began to cascade down in a spectacular curtain of white, showing them exactly what would have happened if they'd left it to mother nature to discharge the snowpack. Kirsten scanned the area and was horrified to see what appeared to be three figures tumbling along with the snow and then disappearing.

"Tim, there's someone out there," she gasped. She grabbed the binoculars and began searching the hillside.

"Where?" he asked.

"I saw three people tumbling along with the slide. They're gone now."

Tim got on the radio and called the artillery operator. "Halt operations! Kirsten saw movement on the slopes."

"We better hurry," Kirsten said, grabbing her gloves and hat. She crashed through the door and down the stairs to the waiting snowmobiles at the base of the tower.

Tim followed on her heels. Speaking into the radio he said, "All teams head to Hill Six. We're looking for three individuals who were caught up in our controlled avalanche. Team one begin at the summit. Team two head midway up. We'll meet you out there."

Kirsten was overcome with guilt. "This is my fault. I should have checked one more time." She had a sick feeling in the pit of her stomach.

Tim didn't answer her and she assumed her voice had been drowned out by the roar of the snowmobiles.

"Kade! Payton! Where are ye?" Bear called into the now silent, frozen landscape. His eyes strained to see beyond the glaring white landscape. He called out to them once again, standing perfectly still listening for even the slightest sound and cursing himself for the danger he'd placed them all in. He gazed down at the spot he'd pulled himself from. They'd been right next to him. Was it possible they landed by his side and he wasn't able to see them? He paced forward, kicking the snow as he went and scanning from left to right hoping he'd spy something that would lead him to his brothers. A sound barely in front of him caught his attention and he noted the movement of the snow and the slightest protrusion of color. He fell to his knees, silently praying and immediately began to frantically dig. Just below the surface he found them. He pulled one and then the other to their feet, brushing the snow from their clothing. "Are ye well?" he asked, looking them both over.

"Aye. Cold." Kade's teeth were chattering loudly as he glanced around. "Where are we?"

"Could the snow have carried us so far? I do no' recognize any of this," Payton said.

"Look at all the trees," Bear said, scanning the area. "I didn't see them last night in the dark. We could have made a fire to keep warm." Even as he said it, he realized something wasn't right. He was sure there were no trees atop Ben Macdhui, but there wasn't time to waste. He had to get Kade to safety.

A buzzing sound in the distance caught their attention as it continued to get louder.

"Come. We must leave." Bear wrapped an arm around Kade and Payton did the same. They trudged off through the snow in search of a familiar landmark; something, anything, that would tell them where they were and allow them to get their bearings.

❄

Kirsten and Tim made it to the spot where she had seen the three figures disappear into the snow. They quickly began the task of locating the victims. They began probing the snow every ten inches in concentric circles.

"I'm not finding anything," Tim said.

"It doesn't seem they had transceivers. I'm not getting any signals." She was getting frustrated and angry at herself. How could she have missed them? She'd seen them clearly enough once the avalanche started. "You'd think that anyone who considered themselves an expert or was crazy enough to buck the rules would know enough to wear a transceiver."

"Keep trying," Tim said as he continued probing the snow.

Team two made their way up to join them and began probing the snow a little further uphill.

"Hey, Tim," Kirsten called.

Tim glanced up from probing. "Yeah?"

"There are footprints over here, leading down the slope." She stood, hands on her hips, staring downhill in hopes of seeing the people they were searching for.

He left what he was doing to join her. "Looks like three people."

"Could they have survived the avalanche?" she asked, feeling suddenly hopeful.

"It's possible."

"I'm going to follow the tracks. I'll radio if I find them."

"Alright, we'll keep searching here."

"I'll go on foot. They can't be too far ahead if it's the group I saw."

"Be careful," Tim cautioned.

Kirsten followed the footprints as they wound their way through the trees and down to a nearby private access road, which had been plowed bright and early that morning, leaving just enough snow for her to continue tracking. She had to make sure they were the people she'd seen. If it was, she could call off the search at the mountain site. She picked up her pace as she walked the access road, frustrated that she wasn't finding anyone. Lined with a thick grove of pine trees, the road curved this way and that, not allowing her to see further than the next hairpin in the road. One thing was for sure, when she found them she was going to give them a piece of her mind. How dare they put themselves and the Search and Rescue crew in danger? She put that out of her head for the time being. She needed to focus and she had no time to let her anger distract her from the mission at hand.

Kirsten loved being part of Search and Rescue. Along with being a member of the ski patrol, it was something she was passionate about. She'd joined as soon as she returned from college. It was something she was good at and nothing felt better to her than helping keep people safe. So, no matter how irritated she was with the people she was tracking, she was a professional and she'd behave like one.

"Kirsten!"

She turned to see Tim heading her way on his snowmobile.

"Did you find anything?" she asked, as he pulled up beside her.

"We were just about to give up when we found a spot where the snow had been disturbed, near where you found the footprints. I don't know how they did it, but they made it out of there."

"Wow! They were lucky."

"Hop on. I'll take you back to your snowmobile."

"Shouldn't we keep searching for them?" She wanted to be one hundred percent sure they were okay and besides she wasn't in any hurry to climb on that snowmobile with Tim.

"It looks like they're fine if they made it this far. Probably just some extreme skiers. We'll probably see their video online later today," he chuckled.

"Still, I'd feel better if we gave it a little more time. If you want to go back, I'll keep looking."

"No. I'm not leaving you alone out here. I'll keep at it if that's what you want."

"It's not what I want, but it's what's right." She held her temper. She was more than capable of doing this job without his help. She didn't need his *protection*. If it was one of her male counterparts, Tim would probably be on his way back to the others instead of staying behind.

"You win." Tim shrugged his shoulders, and winked at her.

She would've rather been searching with anyone else. Not because Tim wasn't good at what he did, but because he would somehow find a way to make this into a date. The wink was a dead giveaway.

They continued scouting the area for another hour both by snowmobile and in some cases on foot. Snow began to fall again, putting an end to their search. Within minutes thick flakes of the white stuff began to cover any tracks that may have been left for them to follow.

"We should head back. Maybe get some hot chocolate at headquarters," Tim said flashing a smile.

This had been a total waste of everyone's time. They'd spent well over two hours searching for these idiots. The searching part was fine, but it also meant she had to endure time alone with Tim and his winks.

They made their way back to the snowmobile. Tim climbed on and motioned for her to hop on.

Kirsten hated to give up, but she was cold and her legs were tired. She climbed on behind Tim.

"Hold on," he instructed.

"I'm fine," she said. Not wanting to wrap her arms around his waist, she gently placed her hands on his sides as he started the drive back.

"What are you doing tonight? I thought we could grab some dinner and then maybe go dancing or something." He shouted over his shoulder so she could hear over the roar of the engine.

"Oh, I don't know. I think they need me at the ski shop tonight," she shouted back.

"I'll call you later then. You own the place. You should be able to take the time off."

"It's our busy season. Especially after a big snowfall like this."

"Okay, but I'll check in with you anyway."

Kirsten didn't say anything even though she knew she should. She couldn't let him continue thinking that they had something, when it was clear to her they didn't. She was such a wimp when it came to things like this. If she wasn't careful, she'd end up marrying him just to spare his feelings. She apparently groaned out loud.

"You okay back there?" Tim asked.

"Fine. Just thinking about something I've got to do."

"Well, let me know if I can help."

They had to find shelter. It was bone-numbing cold and Bear wasn't sure any of them would last much longer if they couldn't sit before a warm fire. This road they trekked along was the finest he'd ever seen. It was cut deep into the side of the mountain with towering trees on either side. It was perfectly flat and almost clear of snow while the sides of the road were piled high with the stuff. Three, perhaps four carts could fit side-by-side across it. Coming around a bend in the road he spied some small dwellings in a field up ahead.

"Look," he pointed towards the cabins.

His brothers stopped long enough to see what he was pointing to and then all three picked up their pace and headed directly for the nearest structure.

"I hope someone's home," Kade said as they approached.

"If not, they'll no' mind if we come in and warm ourselves."

They knocked on the door, but there was no answer.

"Hello?" Bear called, but still nothing. He didn't have to look to know his brothers were freezing and so he tried the door handle and it opened into a large room. Bear was taken aback by what he was seeing. It was different from his home in the Highlands and unlike any he'd seen in his lifetime. His brothers followed him in and closed the door behind them. The walls were perfectly smooth and white with wood trimming the top and bottom. Doors led to other rooms but this wasn't their home, so they stayed where they were, respecting the privacy of those who resided here.

"Does someone live here?" Payton asked.

The interior was clean and neat. Nothing seemed out of place, as if no one had been here in quite some time. "I can no' say." Bear was amazed at all of the unusual things he saw before him. The furnishings were filled with brightly colored pillows made with fabrics he was unfamiliar with. Strange slatted curtains hung on the windows that looked out over the path they'd just walked.

"What is all of this?" Kade asked, sitting on a nearby chair, craning his head to take it all in.

"Here, wrap yerself in this," Bear said, grabbing a blanket from a stack near a small hearth. "I'll start a fire."

Kade took the blanket and did as he was told. Payton followed suit, sitting on a much larger, longer seat that was covered in very fine material and had one part that protruded out into the room. "'Tis like a bed," he said, running he hands over the soft, velvety fabric. "Ye should sit here, Kade. Ye'll be able to lie down and rest properly." He patted the spot next to him.

Kade hoisted himself up from the chair and made his way to Payton, collapsing next to him. Payton made sure he was completely covered by the blanket and placed a pillow beneath his head.

A loud, relieved sigh escaped Kade's lips and both Payton and Bear smiled at the sound.

Wood had been stacked in the hearth, but Bear could find nothing to create the spark needed to start a fire. "Do ye have yer flint?" he asked Payton.

"Aye." Payton reached into his sporran and removed his flint to hand to Bear.

Within a few moments a fire was blazing to life in the hearth. Bear nodded his head in satisfaction. "We'll be warm again soon."

Payton handed him a blanket, which Bear wrapped himself in as he sat next to his brothers. After a moment or two, he stopped shivering and was able to enjoy the warmth seeping into his body. The feeling was returning to his fingers and toes. It seemed such a long time since he'd been comfortably warm. It hardly seemed possible that it had only been a little more than a day since they'd sat around their campfire plotting their revenge on the English.

"Now all we need is food," Kade said.

Bear's thoughts returned to the room and to his brothers. He had been without food for so long that he no longer felt hunger pangs, but Kade was right. They needed sustenance. "We'll warm ourselves first and then I'll go out and see what I can hunt down." For the first time since they'd begun their escape from the dragoons, Bear felt safe. He had no idea where they were or who's cabin they'd stumbled upon, but he was relieved they were out of the cold and that freezing to death was no longer something to fash over.

CHAPTER 2

"Who's there?" a male voice shouted. "We can see the smoke from the chimney, so we ken yer in there."

Bear awoke from a dead sleep. For a moment, he was unsure of his surroundings and reached for his sword. As he looked around he saw that Payton and Kade had done the same, though Kade did not appear strong enough to raise his in defense.

"Ross! Ross, wait! Be careful," a female voice could be heard outside of the cabin.

Bear dropped his blanket and moved towards the door ready to open it, suddenly unsure of what he might find.

Kade and Payton joined Bear at the door. "'Tis Bear Fletcher and me brothers, Kade and Payton. We were cold and seeking shelter."

The door sprang open and they all jumped back, swords at the ready. A tall man with an angry scowl on this face strode in, followed by a wee lass who clung to his back, peeking around from behind him. He could barely see the lass, standing as she was behind a large tree trunk of a man who wore strange trewes and a shirt made from tartan. He didn't appear to be armed, but Bear stood ready to fight if need be.

The group all stood their ground, sizing each other up.

"I be Ross," the tall man said, pushing his way further into the room. "This is me wife, Cassie. Yer on our property." He gazed at the three of them with what appeared to be familiarity, scanning them from head to foot and paying particular attention to their weapons. He reached out a hand towards Bear's sword.

"Apologies to ye," Bear said, pulling the sword in closer to his body and out of the big man's reach.

"There's nae need for weapons, lads," Ross said.

Bear sheathed his sword, but kept his hand close to the hilt. He didn't sense any danger from these two, but one could never be too sure. "We've lost our way and would have frozen to death if it were no' for yer cabin here. We'll be on our way. We are grateful for what little time we were able to spend here."

"Ross, they're Highlanders like you," the woman, Cassie, spoke with a strange accent and seemed surprised that they were Scottish. "Where did you come from?"

"Where are we?" Bear asked, sure he wasn't going to like the answer.

"This is Delight. Didn't you see the sign on your way into town?" Cassie asked.

"Sign?" Bear glanced from Kade to Payton and then back to Ross and Cassie.

"Yeah. 'Welcome to Delight. The most delightful place in the Sierra Nevada.'" The lass tipped her head, placing her hand on her chin as she examined them.

He couldn't keep the puzzlement from his face, noting that Cassie studied him and then, wearing her own puzzled expression, looked to her husband and back again. "You're not from around here." Her eyes flew wide open and she gasped as one hand flew to her lips. "Are you ghosts?"

The brothers all exchanged confused looks. "We no' be ghosts, lass. We're as real as ye." Bear wondered if perhaps they *were* dead and this Delight was the gateway to either heaven or hell or some other place unknown to the living.

"Then how did you get here?" Cassie asked.

"On the snow sliding down Ben Macdhui." Bear looked to his brothers for confirmation.

"'Twas the Grey Man's howl that loosed the snow," Kade added.

Bear gave his brother a warning glare.

"'Twas," Kade said, defying his brother.

"Ben Macdhui? 'Tis in Scotland." Ross seemed excited and in awe of what he'd just learned.

"Aye. We were disoriented by the snow and became lost. We walked until we found this cabin. I must admit things seemed verra different from the way 'twas before we fell. I did no' see one familiar landmark."

"Ross, they didn't walk all the way from Scotland. Something weird is happening here." Cassie furrowed her brow as she continued examining Bear and his brothers.

"Where are we?" Bear asked again, this time feeling a surge of anxiety in his belly.

"Yer going to need to sit for this," Ross said.

Bear motioned to his brothers to sit and he followed suit.

"Yer nae in Scotland anymore. Somehow ye've managed to find yer way across the ocean to us. From an avalanche on Ben Macdhui to an avalanche here in California in what was once the colonies."

He didn't think it was possible to scrunch his eyebrows together any further, but it seemed he could. "We're in the colonies?"

"The colonies." Cassie glanced at Ross before continuing. "If you're not ghosts, it would appear you've time traveled from some time in the past to the year 2019."

"Nae. 'Tis 1747." Bear firmly decreed. These people were obviously quite daft. He glanced at his brothers who wore expressions that said they agreed with his assessment. "We must be on our way." He started towards the door.

"Nae. Dinnae go. I understand yer confusion, but let me explain. Ye say 'tis 1747, aye?"

"Aye," Bear answered.

"I fought at Culloden. Did ye ken any who fought there?"

"Aye. We all fought."

Ross nodded his head and Bear continued. "Once we returned home the English took everything that once was ours. We must return home to claim what is rightfully ours."

"I'm nay sure how ye got here, or why, but I will do me best to help ye."

All five people stood staring at each other. None quite sure what to say. In the silence Kade's belly erupted in a huge growl.

"You must be hungry," Cassie said to Kade. Her face softened, becoming more nurturing as she seemed to notice Kade's frail appearance.

"Aye. Verra," he replied.

"Come with us to our house, we'll get you something hot to eat and we can try to figure this out there."

"Cassie's right," Ross said. "We'll nae settle this here and 'tis best that we feed ye before ye expire. Everything looks better on a full stomach."

"Thank ye," Bear said. "We'll eat and then be on our way. We've nae wish to burden ye."

"It's no trouble at all and you're welcome to stay here in this cabin for now. I think there are some things we need to figure out." Cassie opened the door to the cabin, waiting for them to go ahead of her.

The lass seemed to know something. It couldn't be that they'd traveled through time. It wasn't possible. Still, there had to be some explanation for all of this. He glanced around the small cabin again noting all of the unfamiliar furnishings and other oddities.

They followed Ross and Cassie as they traveled a winding path that led from one cabin to another and then another.

"We rent these out," Cassie explained as they passed. "That's our house over there." She pointed further ahead on the path. Horses grazed in the fading light of the day, poking their noses in the snow in search of green grass.

"I'm going to feed the horses," Ross said as they approached. "I'll see ye inside."

Bear watched as Ross led the horses from the snow covered pasture to a large barn, which lit up brightly as they entered. He had questions aplenty, but he'd wait to ask them.

Reaching the house they mounted the steps. Cassie opened the door and they followed her inside to a large open space. "Welcome," she said.

"Yer home is verra grand," Kade said.

"Oh, thank you. We love it. Ross just finished the carpentry work, so the kitchen is finally done."

All three men nodded their heads. Bear had never seen a home so large. Wide steps led to a covered area that wrapped all the way around. A sloped roof sat atop the two-story building with walls made from long slats of wood that were the color of sunshine. He ran his hand over them surprised at the smooth, even texture. They were all uniform in size and shape unlike anything he'd seen before. He was the chieftain of his small clan. Despite his status, Bear had always been a man of the people. His dwelling was quite modest by comparison. His people were crofters and the homes of their village were more the size of the cabin they'd just left. Ross and Cassie must be verra wealthy.

"Have a seat around the table. I made some nice stew for dinner. It's a perfect night for it. We're expecting more snow tonight." She placed bowls in front of each of them and placed a large, steaming pot in the center of the table. "Help yourselves," she said handing Bear a ladle. "There's some bread warming in the oven. I'll go get it."

"The horses are all settled in for the night," Ross said, entering the house. He walked into the kitchen, grabbed a bowl and sat down at the head of the table.

Cassie placed the hot bread in front of him and he cut it, passing slices to Bear and each of his brothers. "Eat," she ordered as she sat down beside Ross. "I'm curious to know what you think. Since Ross and I moved into the house, I've been cooking more than ever."

"Yer a good cook, Cassie," Ross assured her, taking hold of her hand and giving it a small squeeze.

Cassie responded with a shy smile. "I know you think so, but you *are* a little biased," she replied.

Ross continued holding her hand as the two exchanged love-filled gazes.

"'Tis verra good," Payton said. Bear read the sadness in his eyes. He missed his wife and child. He'd had a life similar to Ross and Cassie before fate cruelly took it away.

"Oh, that's good to know. I've put together some terrible meals, but Ross would never say a word, no matter how bad they were."

"Ye've no need to fear, Lass. We're grateful for the food. 'Tis the best we've had." Bear was pleased when Cassie smiled warmly.

Kade quietly shoveled food into his mouth, looking up every now and then to listen to the conversation around the table.

"Are you feeling better?" Cassie asked him.

He put down his fork long enough to answer. "Aye. The food has helped."

"After dinner I'll take a look at that head wound, if you don't mind. I want to make sure it's stopped bleeding and isn't getting infected. If I don't like the looks of it, we'll take you to the doctor up in Truckee."

"Thank ye." He picked up his fork and dug in again.

They ate their fill in silence from that point on and when they were done, Cassie sent them all into a large room with a roaring fire. "I'll bring you some apple pie," she said.

"Ale?" Ross asked.

"Ross, ale doesn't go with apple pie," she said.

"Nae, but 'tis what they're used to."

"Right," she said, nodding her head in agreement.

Leaving the room, Ross came back with four mugs and placed one in front of each man, keeping one for himself. They nodded their gratitude.

"Ross, why don't you share your story with them," Cassie said as she served them pie.

Everyone's eyes turned to Ross as he spoke. "'Tis quite an unbelievable tale, but I ask ye to keep an open mind as I tell it."

The men all nodded their heads, assuring him of their willingness to believe him.

"Ye see, as I've said, I was at Culloden on that fateful day. I wasnae as lucky as ye. I didnae escape. I was killed along with many others." He stopped, gauging their reactions to what he'd just told them. Their wide eyes and gaping mouths told him that as he suspected, his story was somewhat unbelievable. "I, along with many others haunted the battlefield for well over two hundred years when a wee witch came along and offered me the chance to live again. One good deed would do the trick. She sent me here, where I met Cassie."

"He saved my life that day. It was his good deed."

"I've been here in Delight ever since. I, too, was once consumed with anger and thoughts of revenge, but living here has changed that. It didnae happen overnight, but I be happier now than I've ever been." He glanced at Cassie, who wiped a tear from her cheek.

"I'm sorry. It gets me every time. I can't even imagine what my life would be like without you."

Ross kissed her cheek and took her hand again. He looked to Bear and his brothers. "Ye weren't among the ghosts of Culloden, so tell me about yer journey here," Ross said.

"You say you came from a cave." Cassie leaned forward in her chair, interest clear on her face.

Bear exchanged glances with his brothers before speaking. "We were reaving cattle from the English."

A huge grin broke out on Ross's face. "Go on."

"We were seen and so we had to run. If they caught us we'd either be hung or shipped off to the colonies as slaves. My brothers are no' to blame. 'Twas my idea. We were starving."

"That's terrible," Cassie said. "How could they treat you like that?"

"So ye were reaving cattle," Ross said, "from the English. I'll nae judge on that. I've nae doubt they deserved it." The smirk on his face and the hint of anger in his voice assured Bear that Ross understood exactly what they'd endured.

"Aye. They've taken all we have and left us with nae way to feed ourselves or our families." Bear's gaze landed on Payton. "So ye see, we had to run. They do no' give up easily, so I did the only thing I could think of that would keep them from finding us. We climbed Ben Macdhui."

"We hid in the Grey Man's cave. 'Twas he that caused the snow to take us," Kade said, a note of wonder in his voice.

"Who's the Grey Man?" Cassie asked, stacking the empty bowls and plates in front of her.

"He's a creature or spirit, if ye will, who haunts the mountain," Bear explained.

"Did you see him?" she asked, seeming nervous. "'Cause that would be pretty scary."

"'Tis only a legend," Ross said.

"Nae. He's real. If ye'd been there ye would have heard his mighty howl. He was angry that we were in his cave. 'Twas an unearthly sound that sent us running out into the snow." Kade scrubbed his hands through his hair. It was obvious he'd been shaken by the whole ordeal.

"Well, at least you're safe now," Cassie said.

"Aye, but we must get back," Bear stated.

"Why? You'll love it here. Just ask Ross." She looked to her husband.

"Cassie's right. There's nae reason for ye to go back unless yer leaving a wife or child behind. And even then, I dinnae ken how ye'd be able to do it."

Bear looked to Payton and saw the blood drain from his face. Kade shifted to place a hand on his shoulder, but Payton didn't seem to notice.

"Nae. We have nae wives or children, but our neighbors and friends are struggling. I must get back to my clan."

"Ye said yerself, if yer caught it'll likely be the end of ye," Ross pressed.

"Still. I feel we must try. We can no' give up and let the Sassenachs take our land from us."

"Well, like it or not, they do," Cassie said.

The room fell silent as all eyes turned her way.

"It's true. Tell them, Ross."

Ross nodded his confirmation. "The clans were disbanded. Our way of life destroyed. No more Highland dress. Weapons were banned. Everything from the dirk to the broadsword were outlawed. Scotland was completely under English rule and that has never changed in all these years. The Jacobite cause was defeated, never to return. Many a Highlander went on to fight for the English in the battle for the colonies. A battle that the colonies won, securing their independence from England and becoming the United States of America." Ross smiled at this last part.

"How do ye ken this?" Bear couldn't believe his ears. How could it possibly be true?

"It's history. It's already happened," she answered.

Bear had a sick feeling in the pit of his belly. This couldn't be. Cassie must be mistaken. "We can go back and change things. Defeat our enemies."

"I understand how badly you want to change history, to help your friends. I just don't know that you could possibly get back." The sad look on Cassie's face didn't bode well for them.

Bear was ready to argue with her when he caught sight of Kade. Despite the good meal, he was still looking unsteady. He needed time to heal and Bear wasn't going anywhere without his brothers. "We'll stay here for a while, build up our strength once again and then be on our way home. Of course, we'll work for our keep. Anything ye need, we'll happily oblige ye."

"Oh, believe me. There's plenty for you to do around here." Cassie's face brightened. "The town's preparing for our winter festival and having three more handsome highlanders around will be perfect for attracting visitors."

"I'm nae sure why, but the ladies of this time seem quite taken with Highlanders." Ross winked at his wife.

"How so?"

"Ye'll soon find out. We'll take ye into town tomorrow. For now, relax and enjoy yer first night in Delight."

"I'll walk ye back to the cabin," Ross said, putting on a warm coat and pulling a strange stick from his pocket. A light beam emanated from it and Bear couldn't help himself. He reached out and took it from Ross.

"What is this?" he asked, turning it this way and that, amazed at the powerful light that nearly blinded him when he tried to examine it.

"'Tis a flashlight. Much better than a torch or a lantern."

"Truly," Kade said as he took it from his brother and pointed it towards the woods that backed onto the land surrounding them. "I can see into the trees and they're so verra far away." He handed it back to Ross.

"I'll be sure to get one for each of ye. They come in handy when yer walking around out here in the dark."

"Thank ye. Ye've been most kind." Luck had been on their side when they'd stumbled upon this cabin. The generous spirit of their hosts wasn't something he was likely to forget.

"We're brothers of a sort. Culloden will always bind us to one another."

"Aye. We barely escaped with our lives." Bear looked off into the distance remembering that terrible day. "And ye did no'." He had been stunned by this news, by Ross's tale of magic and witchcraft, but why should he be. If they'd actually time traveled from the past then anything was possible. Anything at all.

Ross was nodding his head in agreement.

"And yet, here ye are."

"Happy to be alive and happy to have Cassie by my side," Ross said.

They'd reached the cabin and Ross led the way up the steps and inside. With the flick of a switch, the room was ablaze with light.

"Flashlights?" Kade asked.

"Nae. Lightbulbs."

Bear nodded along with his brothers at this news. It was best just to accept the fact that everything they would see from this day forward would be unlike anything they'd ever seen before.

"There are four bunk beds in the back room behind the kitchen." Ross walked as he spoke and the brothers followed along behind him. They hadn't taken the time to look around earlier, not wanting to overstep their welcome when they found no one at home. "Extra blankets and pillows are here and ye turn the lights on and off like this." He flicked another switch and the lights in the room went on and then with another flick they were off. Bear watched as each of his brothers tried it and came away with huge ear-to-ear grins on their faces. It did his heart good to see it. They hadn't smiled in a verra long time. "Sleep as late as ye like tomorrow morning and come to the house when ye wake, or I'll come get ye. We'll go into town and introduce ye to everyone. We'll have to come up with a story for yer sudden appearance, but Cassie will help with that." He walked back out into the front room, showing them the kitchen and bathroom and how it all worked. "I don't think I've forgotten anything, so I'll bid ye good night. Oh, and tomorrow we'll be sure to get ye some warmer clothes."

"Good night," Bear closed the door then looked down at his threadbare clothing and the old fur skin he'd wrapped himself in. It amazed him how they'd gone from the brink of death to all of this. He was thankful that his brothers would be safe. It seemed fate had intervened just in the nick of time. "Come," he beckoned to his brothers and as they got close he wrapped an arm around each of them, hugging them as tightly as he could, feeling the bones of them where muscle had once been. "I'm sorry," was all he could manage to say as his voice choked with tears.

"Bear, do no' blame yerself. We do no'. We'd gladly follow ye again, no matter the outcome," Payton said, pulling away and gazing into Bear's eyes.

"He's right," Kade added. "Think on it. If we had no' followed ye, we never would have found this place. 'Tis the best we could've hoped for. I, for one, am happy to be here."

"As I am," Payton added.

Bear straightened his spine and swiped at his eyes with the backs of his hands before any errant teardrops could fall. Clearing his throat, he said. "We should get some sleep. I believe we'll need to be well rested for whatever tomorrow may bring."

CHAPTER 3

a sleepy-eyed Cassie opened the door to where Bear and his brothers waited on her front porch.

"Wow! You're here early," she said, rubbing her eyes and yawning.

"We're sorry, lass. Would ye like us to come back later," Bear asked.

"No, of course not, come in." She held the door open for them to pass.

"Good morn to ye," Kade said as he entered. Bear couldn't help but note how much better he looked.

"Make yourselves at home in the living room. I'll get some coffee started and while it's brewing I'll get dressed and wake Ross."

Bear nodded to his brothers and all three sat on the large, over-stuffed cushions of the sofa. "Thank ye, lass."

"I'll be right back," she said as she finished puttering around in the kitchen and then ran upstairs.

"We're too early," Payton said, his voice barely above a whisper.

"The sun's up," Kade said. "I thought sure they'd be awake and waiting for us."

Ross strode down the steps. "We sleep a little later here. I'm going to feed the horses and let them out. Looks like the snow passed us by last night. 'Tis a good thing. We'll have time to clean up after the last storm."

"Can we help ye?" Bear asked. "'Tis something we can do in the mornings if ye like."

"Aye. Come along. I'll show ye where we keep the feed."

The three men followed Ross across the yard to the stable. Bear was immediately awestruck by what he was seeing. Neat stalls lined up one next to the other with ornate wood and iron doors that opened onto each stall. Inside were the horses they'd seen last night in the field. It was quite warm in the stable, unlike the freezing temperatures they'd just left outdoors. Bear watched as Ross hit something on the wall that closed the large barn door behind them. The sweet smell of hay wafted to his nose and for a moment he was back home caring for his own horse, when he'd had one. The sadness he felt remembering his noble steed was still strong. His constant companion from the moment the colt was born until the day that the dragoons led him away. Bear had wanted to stop them, but Kade and Payton held him back, preventing him from becoming another casualty among their clan. He ran his hand over the soft nose of the horse closest to him.

"That's Evergreen," Ross volunteered. "We call her Evie."

Her warm breath blew out onto Bear's hand and he gently reciprocated by blowing small puffs of his own breath into her nose, introducing himself to her in the way that horses did. She nickered to him and the knot in his heart slowly began to melt away.

"She likes ye," Ross said. "I'd ask ye if ye ride, but I can see from watching ye that yer familiar with horses."

"Aye," Bear acknowledged.

"I'll need help exercising this lot. Perhaps ye'd like to help with that."

"I'd be happy to." He ran his hand down Evie's neck. "Would ye like that?"

Again, she nickered to him, almost as if she understood what he was saying to her.

"The feed is back here," Ross continued walking down the aisle, followed by the brothers. "The stalls are cleaned every morning and evening. Manure forks are here along with buckets."

"What about water?" Kade asked.

"We have automatic waterers."

"Automatic?"

"Aye. They fill themselves."

Eyebrows popped up and mouths gaped at this announcement.

"Ye've a lot to learn and ye willnae learn it all in one day. I'll do my best to help ye. If ye have questions, ask me or Cassie. 'Twill be best to keep yer background a secret from the others as we've done with mine. We'll come up with a story for ye over breakfast." Ross handed them each a fork and bucket. "The sooner we finish, the sooner we'll eat."

They divided up the stalls and were finished feeding and cleaning in no time at all. Leaving the warmth of the barn, the cold hit them hard. Bear wrapped his arms around himself as did the others. Ross was dressed in much warmer clothes and seemed to tolerate the freezing temperature much better.

Entering the house once again, Bear said, "'Tis a wonder how warm yer home is... and the barn. Not a draft to be felt."

"In our time, things were different," Ross said. "Ye must remember that almost three hundred years have passed. Everything has changed and improved."

"Ye must share the information with me. When we go back, mayhap we can make things better for ourselves and our neighbors."

Ross tipped his head, one eyebrow cocked as a quizzical expression passed over his face. "Why would ye nae stay here? I believe ye'd be much happier."

"'Tis no' our home," was Bear's reply. How could he ever forgive himself for deserting his people? Their village had been decimated and most had moved on, leaving what had once been their beloved home to find work. All he wanted was for this nightmare to end. For everything to go back to the way it had once been. He just wanted to go home.

Ross shrugged his shoulders and headed for the long table where food had been laid out for them along with a steaming hot beverage that was blacker than pitch, having a distinct odor he recognized as coffee. He'd smelled it once on a journey he'd made to Edinburgh on clan business. The distinct scent stuck with him conjuring memories of that day. It wasn't something widely available to the people of his clan. They drank tea and he was sure that even if they'd been able to have coffee it wouldn't have swayed them from their beloved tea. He'd say tea was his preference, but he was curious about trying this coffee he'd heard so much about.

The food on the table seemed to be typical breakfast fare. Platters of eggs and bannocks were joined by a heaping pile of bacon and frosted sweet rolls. He was happy to know that food was still very much the same because breakfast had always been his favorite meal of the day. Lately it was the only meal and at that quite skimpy.

He watched as Kade's eyes took in the wealth of food set before them before digging in and taking a bit of everything. "Slow down there, brother. Leave some for the rest of us."

"It's fine," Cassie said. "We've got plenty and besides, you all look as though you could use a good meal or ten." She smiled warmly at them before turning back to the kitchen where she gathered more food to bring to the table.

"A feast fit for a king," Ross said.

"Today we've got four kings," Cassie teased. "What did you think of our barn?"

"We've never seen anything like it," Bear answered. "A dream come true for any horse."

"Evie took a liking to him," Ross said, nodding his head towards Bear.

"She's so sweet," Cassie said. "Easy to love."

"I can see that," Bear said.

"Well, eat up. We're going into town today. I thought we'd say that you were cousins of Ross and you were visiting from Scotland. What do you think of that?"

"Makes sense," Ross said.

The brothers nodded their agreement as their mouths were too full to say even a word.

"Good."

They drove into town in what Cassie called a truck. Ross and she sat in front and the three brothers squeezed into the back seat, examining every button and lever and running their hands over the leather seats. It felt strange being enclosed in such a small space, but as they went, Bear noted a number of other *trucks* on the road with them. They came in various shapes, sizes and colors. The speed at which they traveled left little time to see what they were passing. Buildings and houses went by in a blur.

Ross pulled the truck into a space in front of a row of buildings that seemed to house shops of varying kinds. The men pulled themselves from the truck, stretching their limbs now that they had room to move. Bear glanced up and down the lane, noting the *paved* road was bordered by paved walkways. It reminded him in some ways of the times he'd ventured in to Edinburgh where the shops were so close together that they shared walls. Many of these buildings housed balconies that looked out over the main street. People were walking around carrying packages as they did their shopping.

They followed Ross and Cassie as they headed into one of the buildings.

"Rose, I want you to meet our guests," Cassie said as they entered a sweet smelling shop filled with mouthwatering treats. "This is Bear Fletcher and his brothers, Kade and Payton. They're Ross's cousins and they're here visiting with us from Scotland."

"Welcome," Rose said, coming out from behind the glass cases. "How long are you here for?" she asked.

"It's open ended at the moment," Cassie interrupted before they could speak.

"This is wonderful," Rose bubbled. "They'll be a perfect draw for the winter festival, don't you think?"

"I do," Cassie said and then turned to the men. "Rose has the best bakery in the Sierra Nevadas. Everything is delicious."

"I've been working on my scones and shortbread, now that we're trying to promote a Highland vibe here in Delight."

Bear looked at his brothers, who seemed equally puzzled by everything Rose had just shared.

"They're nae used to yer words, Rose. They're much the same as I was when I first arrived."

Rose laughed. "I'll keep that in mind. Are you hungry?" she asked.

Bear noted that Kade was just about to speak. He had a ravenous look in his eye and Bear didn't wish him to be rude, so he spoke first. "Nae. We've just eaten. Cassie fed us well."

"Come back later. You can try my Scottish treats and let me know what you think."

"'Twill be our pleasure," Bear answered for all three.

"Are you showing them around our little village?" Rose asked.

"We are, but first I've got to get my shop open. I'll leave the introductions to Ross."

"Good meeting you, and Cassie, I'll be over in a little while with our tea," Rose said.

"I can't wait to try the new blends you just got in."

"You'll love them."

Once in the bookstore, Ross showed them around. When they got to the Highlander Romance section of the shop as Ross called it, Bear and his brothers were taken aback as they examined the covers of the books Ross said were Cassie's best sellers.

"Ross, when you're done, you should take them around town. Introduce them to everyone."

"I will," he answered.

The door to the shop opened as someone entered. Whoever it was, they were so bundled up in their clothing that Bear couldn't see if it was a man or woman.

"Hey, Cassie... Ross."

It was a woman. She pushed the hood back from her head and

Bear was surprised to see a rosy cheeked lass with lovely sky blue eyes and soft golden hair.

"Kirsten!" Cassie rushed over to give her a hug.

"I'm sorry I couldn't make dinner last night. I hope you didn't go to too much trouble cooking for me."

"No worries. We had plenty of company last night so nothing went to waste. From your phone call it sounds like you had a crazy day yesterday."

"I'm so mad at myself for not double checking before we started the slide. I'm usually so careful."

"What happened?"

"Three idiots appeared out of nowhere as the slide came barreling downhill."

"Oh, no," Cassie glanced at Ross and then at Bear.

"Lucky for them they somehow managed to get away. Tim and I searched for them until the snow started falling and then we had to give up."

Bear cleared his throat. "It seems we're the three idjits ye saw."

Cassie was standing behind Kirsten shaking her head at him. Should he not have spoken?

"You! What were you thinking?" Kirsten's voice went from sweet to harsh in a matter of seconds. "You could have been killed. You could have gotten the search and rescue team killed."

"But everyone was fine, right?" Cassie asked.

"That's beside the point," Kirsten barked, turning her head towards her. "It was an incredibly tense situation and whether or not anyone was hurt, it was dangerous. The team spent a couple hours searching the mountain, not to mention that they couldn't open half the ski runs until we finished the search and made sure the mountain was safe."

"Of course," Cassie said. She mouthed the word sorry to Bear.

"How did you get up there? Helicopter? Are you extreme skiers?" she asked Bear, fire in her eyes as she peppered him with questions.

He hesitated for only a moment, unsure which question to answer first.

"Well, are you going to answer me?"

"Aye." He had no idea what extreme skiers were, but he was confident he and his brothers were not. Helicopter? Another unfamiliar word. He'd been warned not to tell anyone where they'd come from, so he chose his words carefully. "We were on foot when the snow overtook us."

"On foot!" She seemed even angrier if that was possible. "So I guess all the warning signs we have posted along the trails just don't apply to you guys. You really are an idiot, aren't you?" Her hands went to her hips. He felt the full fury of her disapproval.

"Kirsten, I don't think we need to insult anyone," Cassie interrupted.

"No, the lass is right to call me an idjit. 'Twas my fault that we were all in danger. My brothers merely followed me. They are no' to blame."

"You know, it really annoys the hell out of me when people like you scoff at the rules and regulations." She glared at him, which made her eyes even more beautiful as they darkened to sapphire. Kirsten seemed to take a brief moment to shake the anger out of herself before turning to Cassie. "I've got to get back to work. I just wanted to apologize for last night."

"It's okay. Maybe you can come by tonight," Cassie said.

"We'll see. I'll talk to you later." With that she was out the door before anyone could say another word.

"Wow! I'm so sorry. She's usually much nicer than that," Cassie said, breaking the shocked silence.

"She seems quite passionate," Bear said. When he'd first seen her, he'd appreciated her sweet, cherubic face, when that was replaced with a fiery side, it sparked something in him he'd not felt in a long time.

"She is, but don't judge her on what just happened. She's the best person you'd ever want to meet. If she comes for dinner tonight you'll see a whole different side of her."

Bear was skeptical that she'd be any more receptive to him tonight than she had been just now.

"I'm going to show them around, love. Do ye have a list for me to take care of?" Ross said.

"Of course," she pulled a piece of paper covered in small writing from her bag. On top of this, they're going to need warmer clothes," Cassie offered.

"Where should we go?"

"The ski shop, but maybe not today," a nervous smile crossed her lips as she gazed at Bear and his brothers. "Kirsten owns the ski shop. You should probably avoid her for now. She'll get over it soon enough... I hope."

"We'll be back soon," Ross said, leading them out the door.

he absolute nerve of those three, Kirsten thought as she trudged to her shop through the snow, hopping over snowbanks as she crossed the street. Some of Delight's residents were already out shoveling their sidewalks and the snow plow had made one or two passes down the main street. As she reached the ski shop, Kirsten became painfully aware of the fact that it was her job to shovel this time. She, Amy and Sue took turns shoveling after each storm. It wasn't something she was looking forward to, but it might help her burn off some of the irritation she was feeling about yesterday's near calamity. She'd been so irate on meeting the men, that she hadn't even asked who they were or where they'd come from. They were brothers, that much she had caught. The oldest had done all the talking. He'd bristled at her tone, but had remained civil and even taken responsibility. His chocolatey brown eyes and long dark hair were something she was sure she wouldn't forget. Under normal circumstances, she'd say he was delicious to look at. The sound of his deep voice and thick Scottish accent would be irresistible if he hadn't already proven himself to be someone who had no care for his own safety, the safety of others, or the rules. If she'd met him at any other time, instead of yelling at him, she'd be flirting with him. She kicked at the nearest snowbank, stubbing her toe. "Ouch! Stupid!"

She put her key in the lock of the door to the ski shop, as she glanced back over her shoulder. Ross was leading the three men down the street. It was obvious from his gestures that he was giving them a tour of their little ski village. For a moment her eyes met Mr. Tall, Dark and Handsome. She quickly turned away, slamming into the door, which she hadn't yet opened. "Grrr..."

Once safely inside the store, she peeked out the window and watched the men until they were out of sight. "I hope he doesn't bring them in here," she said to herself as she turned on the lights and turned up the heat. "That sidewalk isn't going to shovel itself." She grabbed the shovel from behind the counter and went back outside into the biting cold to clear the sidewalk. Within a few minutes, she was toasty warm from her exertions.

"Kirsten!" Avery Winters, the inn owner rushed across the street.

"Hey, Avery," Kirsten stopped shoveling to greet her. "You look excited about something. What's up?"

"Did you see them?" she asked.

Kirsten had a sneaking suspicion she knew exactly who Avery was talking about, but she'd pretend she didn't. Why take away her friend's excitement at telling her? "Who?"

"The three handsome Highlanders with Ross. I wonder what they're doing here."

"I have no idea," she said. She really wanted to say, *causing trouble, breaking the rules and endangering people's lives,* but she didn't.

"I hope they're staying for The WinterFest. They'll be good for business."

"I'm sure they will." Kirsten threw a shovelful of snow up onto the snowbank.

"You don't seem too excited about it," Avery said. "What's wrong?"

"Oh, nothing much."

"It's the shoveling, isn't it? Do you want me to help?"

"No, I've got this. It's not my favorite job, but I can do it. Besides, don't you have to shovel in front of the inn?"

Avery's face lit up. "Justin shoveled for me."

"The new guy at the hardware store?"

"Uh-huh. Flannel never looked so good."

"Avery Winters, you've got a crush," Kirsten teased.

"Have you seen the man? He's hot, hot, hot!"

Kirsten couldn't help but laugh at her friend's obvious lust for this guy. It wasn't often that new residents moved to town and when they did everyone knew all about them in no time, especially if he was a good looking, single guy. There simply weren't enough of those to go around.

"Are you laughing at me?"

"Of course I am," Kirsten chuckled. "I love your enthusiasm."

"Yeah, we'll see who's laughing when I marry this guy."

"Getting a little ahead of yourself aren't you? Have you even gone on a date?"

"I think shoveling qualifies. You should try it some time."

Kirsten raised her eyebrows at that one.

"What about Tim? I bet he'd be happy to shovel for you."

"I know he would be, but I'm trying to *not* encourage him." Another shovelful went over the snowbank. "He's a nice guy and all, but he's not what I want."

"Does he know that?"

"No. I can't seem to bring myself to tell him. I don't want to hurt his feelings." She pushed the last bits of snow towards the curb and leaned on her shovel. Unzipping the top of her parka, she could feel the heat she had generated wafting up and out.

"I better get back to the inn. My guests will be wondering where I am," she giggled. "Talk to you later."

Kirsten watched her friend hurry back across the street, knowing that if Avery put her mind to it, Justin wouldn't know what hit him.

She thought about Tim and what she needed to do. This subject depressed her. She had a guy who was ready, willing and able to be her man, but she didn't want him. There was no spark there. To be honest she hadn't ever felt that spark, that connection with any of the men she'd dated and she was beginning to wonder if she ever would. It was ski season though and anything was possible. People were always coming in from out of town. Maybe she'd get lucky and the man of her dreams would be one of them.

A familiar car pulled into the diagonal parking space in front of her store. "Ugh!" Kirsten muttered under her breath.

"Hey, little lady, you already shoveled. I thought you might need some help."

"I'm not helpless, Tim." She turned and entered the shop with Tim right behind her. She unzipped her parka and he was right there helping her out of it. She rolled her eyes heavenward and was glad he was behind her and couldn't see.

"Where is everyone?" he asked, glancing around the shop.

"Not here," she answered.

"I can see that. Aren't Amy and Sue working today?"

"Amy will be in after lunch and Sue is taking the day off."

"You should fire them," he said.

Kirsten bristled at this. He was sticking his nose in where it didn't belong. "They're my business partners." She turned to face him. "I have no reason to fire them."

"Why are you always the one who has to work? I wanted to take you out last night for a nice dinner, but you had to work." He seemed quite peeved about the whole thing.

"Look, even if I didn't have to work last night, I wouldn't have been able to join you for dinner. I was invited to Cassie's and I had to cancel that, too."

Tim wasn't letting this drop. "It's not fair that you're always the one who has to work. Here you are again this morning. If they were my partners, I'd be having words with them."

Kirsten really didn't appreciate him inserting himself into her business. It was clear to her that he didn't like her friends and he thought they were taking advantage of her. "You have no idea what you're talking about. We all work equally hard to make this shop profitable. I don't work any more or less than they do and even if I did, it would be because I want to."

"Okay, okay. No need to get testy with me. I'll mind my own business. I'm just worried about you. You were up early yesterday morning helping to clear the slopes and then you spent the rest of the day searching high and low for those skiers. I don't want to see you work yourself to death."

"Thank you and I'm sorry. My morning got off to a bad start."

"Really? Why?"

"I ran into our three avalanche survivors."

Tim went into Search and Rescue mode. "Where? I want to talk to them."

"You don't have to. I gave them a piece of my mind. They're friends of Ross's, I think. I didn't really wait around for proper introductions."

"Did you tell them that what they'd done was dangerous?"

"Of course I did. I explained to them that their thoughtless actions had endangered not only themselves, but the team."

"I should talk to them to make sure they really understand."

"I made sure they understood." Did he think she was stupid or something?

"Right."

"They won't do anything that foolish again. They're brothers and the oldest took the blame for it."

"Still, I better not see them around."

"You will, so you better keep your temper under control." Kirsten knew Tim could get pretty angry with skiers who left the trails or who recklessly put other skiers in harm's way as they tore downhill. Not that it was a bad thing, but he was over-the-top sometimes. This was a tourist town, after all. They got skiers of all abilities. He really needed to find a better way to deal with his frustration because they were all working hard to attract more people to the town, not scare them away. This was just another difficult conversation she needed to have with him. She was so lost in her own thoughts that she didn't realize he had moved closer to her until he touched her shoulder reminding her that he was there.

"Hey, I'm going to the bakery. Do you want me to bring you back anything? Coffee? Tea?"

"No, thanks. You don't need to hang around here with me. I've got to go over the books. Tax season will be here in no time so I want to get a head start."

"Are you sure? I can take care of customers while you work."

"Nope." She tried to keep her voice light. They needed to talk, but not here and definitely not right now. "This is your free time and you should be doing something fun."

"Alright. Maybe we can have dinner later."

"Sorry. I'm having dinner with Cassie and Ross tonight." She'd told Cassie she'd let her know, but Tim made up her mind for her.

"Okay. I'll see you tomorrow then."

Kirsten walked him to the door. "Bye." Much to her chagrin he leaned in to kiss her cheek before heading off.

A heavy sigh escaped her lips. She had to stop being a chicken and do something about this.

CHAPTER 4

"I'm surprised to see you," Cassie said. "I thought you'd probably have plans with Tim. You know you could have brought him with you." Cassie held the door open as Kirsten entered.

"We're not dating, Cassie." Kirsten took off her snowy boots and placed them on a mat by the door. A chill enveloped her feet and she shook each of them in an effort to get her blood flowing.

"Oh, sorry. I thought you were getting serious." She motioned for Kirsten to follow her.

"Tim thinks we are." And that was the problem. He seemed to have convinced everyone, including her best friend, that they were an item.

"That's probably where I got it from." Cassie looked appropriately embarrassed.

Kirsten handed Cassie a bottle of wine and took her jacket off.

"Thanks. I'll open it so we can have a glass." She took Kirsten's jacket and the bottle as she left the room.

Kirsten took a seat on the sofa facing the fireplace, holding her feet straight out in front of her. Wood crackled and sparked in the blazing fire. The warmth felt good. She'd known Cassie since she was a child, but they hadn't been close growing up. Circumstances had led them in different directions. Cassie had married and divorced her childhood sweetheart and Kirsten had been in a hurry to get to the big city where she was convinced she belonged. Over the course of the last year, as they both led the charge to get more tourists to their small town, they'd gotten quite close. Now Kirsten couldn't imagine her life without Cassie in it. "Where's Ross?"

"He's taking care of the horses. He'll be back in a bit," Cassie called from the kitchen.

"I wanted to apologize for the scene at your shop this morning," Kirsten said as Cassie returned.

Cassie handed Kirsten a glass of wine and joined her by the fire. "That's hardly what I would call a scene."

"It was for me. I don't know what came over me. It was just that they could've been killed. I wanted them to know how serious it was."

Cassie reached over to comfort her with a pat on her arm. "They know," Cassie assured her. "They are new in town and we didn't have a chance to explain about the trails…" her voice trailed off as she fidgeted with her shirt.

"What's up? Is there something you're not telling me?"

"They're joining us for dinner."

"Oh!" How embarrassing was that going to be?

"I know. I should have told you, but I wasn't sure you were actually going to show up. Don't be mad at me."

"I'm not mad." She wasn't. She was actually just tired from her long day and, to be honest, relieved that she'd had an excuse to avoid Tim. "I didn't know I was going to have to socialize. I was hoping for a quiet evening with you and Ross. Are you sure they even want to see me?"

"It'll be fine. They're great guys."

"Maybe I should start by asking how you know them."

"They're Ross's cousins. They're from Scotland. Here for a visit." Cassie was fidgeting with her shirt again and though she was answering Kirsten's question, seemed a bit distracted.

"How long are they staying?"

"It's indefinite for now."

The door opened followed by a blast of cold air as Ross and his

41

cousins entered. These guys took their Scottish heritage seriously. They were all dressed in kilts as they had been earlier in the day. The older brother had some sort of fur draped around his shoulders. There was something raw and rugged about them. In fact, if Kirsten blurred out all the modern conveniences, they looked as though they were from another time.

"Kirsten!" Ross exclaimed. "I'm so happy ye could make it."

"Me, too," she half-lied. This would be alright. She could keep her irritation to herself. She was sure of it.

"Ye remember me cousins, though I dinnae think we made proper introductions." Ross grinned at her, clearly enjoying this. During the last year Kirsten had a chance to get to know him. He was a great partner for Cassie and did everything he could to help out around town. She couldn't be happier to see her friend with someone like him after what she had been through. Although at the moment, he was being equal parts annoying and charming. "This is Bear, Kade and Payton. Gentlemen, may I introduce Kirsten Hunter." Ross did some sort of old-fashioned bow and Kirsten couldn't help but roll her eyes at him.

"Have a seat, lads. Can I get ye some ale? Wine? A wee dram of whisky?"

"Whisky," Bear answered, giving Kirsten the same side-eyed glance she was giving him. "Me brothers will have the same."

They nodded their heads as he spoke.

"How about ye, lass?" Ross asked.

"We've got wine." Cassie held up her glass so Ross could see. "But while you're at it, could you get the bottle. I left it in the kitchen and I think I'm ready for more. Kirsten?"

"I'm good for now."

The men took seats on the sofa with Kirsten. Bear sat next to her, his leg brushing hers as he settled in. Her belly did a little flip-flop at his touch.

"My apologies, lass. I did no' mean to encroach on ye." He moved slightly, relieving the pressure of thigh against thigh.

"Thanks," Kirsten said, taking a gulp of her wine. "So, Cassie tells me you're from Scotland."

Bear glanced at Cassie who nodded ever so slightly at him. *Strange,* Kirsten thought.

"Aye, we are."

"And you're here from Scotland for an indefinite stay?"

Again the glance and nod. What on earth was going on?

"Aye, we are."

"I've never been to Scotland. I hear it's beautiful there."

"Aye, 'tis."

"Interesting," she said. He didn't seem to have a whole lot to say and as for his brothers, they'd been silent since they arrived. They didn't seem like the extreme sport enthusiasts she had met in the past. They seemed more quiet, circumspect. They weren't even dressed appropriately for the weather. Why would they be wandering around on the mountain after a fresh snowfall? Kirsten couldn't help but wonder how it was that the three of them ended up in the middle of her controlled avalanche.

Ross brought glasses, a bottle of whisky and the open bottle of wine. He poured more wine for Cassie and whisky for each of the men and then one for himself. "*Slainte.*"

They all raised their glasses and then took a drink.

"I know that when I saw you earlier today I was pretty upset. I don't usually yell at people the first time I meet them. I'm still confused about why you were out there. On these hillsides, fresh snow can turn deadly. Have you ever seen an avalanche before?" she asked.

"Aye," the younger brother answered. "'Tis how we…"

"…know how dangerous they can be," Bear finished for his brother. Kade looked at him, then at Kirsten and nodded.

She narrowed her eyes at Bear, who nervously shifted in his seat.

"Really, it was our fault," Cassie said. "We should have warned them, but they were out exploring before we had a chance. They would never purposely put themselves or anyone else in danger." Cassie gave Bear a meaningful look.

"Aye. Apologies to ye, lass," Bear added.

What was up with everyone? Kirsten couldn't be sure of it, but her gut told her that there was something fishy going on here. The younger brother had almost slipped up and Bear had jumped in to rescue him. Even Cassie was trying to smooth things over. Her curiosity was piqued. No matter how hard they tried to hide it, Kirsten would get to the bottom of whatever it was they were trying to cover up.

The lass was on to them. Bear was going to have to talk to Kade about being careful with his words. Payton wasn't a concern. He had very little to say about anything at all.

"Kirsten is a member of the search and rescue for our mountain," Cassie said.

"And the ski patrol," Ross added.

"And she's part owner of the ski shop in town."

"I like to keep busy," Kirsten interjected.

"Yer important to yer clan," Bear said.

"I don't have a clan," Kirsten replied.

"Sure you do," Cassie interrupted. "We're your clan. Everyone in Delight is your clan."

Bear glanced at Ross.

"'Tis nae the same as back home, ye ken."

Bear nodded his understanding. He still hadn't come to grips with the fact that they were in the colonies. Ross had shown him a map and told him they were in a state called California, but it all seemed too fantastical to him. How could he be so far away from all that was familiar to him. The thought occurred to him that perhaps they'd all died in the snow slide. If so, he didn't feel any less alive than he had. And if they really had time traveled as Ross and Cassie believed, could they ever go home and how?

"Dinner's almost ready. I'm going to set the table."

"I'll help," Kirsten said as she followed Cassie into the dining room.

Bear followed her with his eyes. "The women of this time are verra different."

"They're free to be who and what they wish," Ross explained. "I must admit that I enjoy it."

"I'm with ye," Kade said, a sudden smile appearing on his face. "I believe I'll enjoy it verra much."

Ross chuckled and raised his glass once again, "Here's to the lassies of this time."

They all drank, but Payton. He sat sullenly, staring into the fire. Bear felt the heavy burden of responsibility for all he had been through. He would have to speak with him when they got back to the cabin. The grieving process had only just begun and the road ahead would be long. Bear hoped Payton would make his way past the twists and turns and finally come to a place where he was at peace. Then maybe love would find him again.

"We're planning a WinterFest, here in Delight. 'Twill be the first one, but hopefully nae the last." Ross placed his glass on a side table and sat in the chair by it. "Ye lads have arrived in the nick of time."

"How so?" Kade asked.

"Ye see, when I arrived in Delight, 'twas a sad time for the village. Their businesses were suffering. No one came to their shops or their inn. Cassie had the idea that I could help draw people to town. 'Tis something we've been working on since I arrived. Now yer here and there are more of us."

"How do ye help?" Bear wondered.

"I greet people around town. I spend time at the book shop with Cassie." He winked. "The women love us."

"Aye. I saw the books."

"So we've created a theme for Delight. One that involves High-landers. And it's worked. We've plans for events throughout the year. The WinterFest is next and will take much planning on everyone's part. We'll fill the inn, the cottages we've got on the property and we'll use the barn for concerts and dancing."

"And how can we help?" Bear asked.

"I'm only one man and I cannae be everywhere at one time, so if ye can help greet people and show them around our village, 'twould be a great thing. Cassie will tell ye all about it over dinner."

The final place setting was on the table and Kirsten turned to Cassie with a furrowed brow.

"What's wrong? Are we missing something?"

"No. Nothing's missing. I was just… never mind."

"I can't possibly never mind when I see that face of yours."

Cassie could read her like a book, so she'd never been successful in hiding anything from her and she probably shouldn't try now. "I don't know what to do. I feel like such a terrible person."

"If you're talking about yelling at the guys earlier, I think they're over it." She picked up a glass examining it closely before placing it back on the table.

"I do feel terrible about that, but that's not what's bothering me. It's…" she hesitated momentarily before blurting out, "Tim."

"Tim? What did you do to him?" Cassie asked, tipping her head and giving Kirsten a stern look.

"Nothing… yet."

"And what is it that you're going to do that makes you a terrible person?"

"I've got to tell him I'm not interested in him, but I don't know how. I feel overwhelmed, like he's suffocating me. We're not even officially a couple, but I'm pretty sure he believes we are."

"I don't think there's any way you get out of this without hurting his feelings, but you can't stick with it just to keep him happy. It's okay to think about what's right for you."

"You're right, but I have to work with him. It will be unbelievably awkward having to see him on a regular basis."

"You are both adults. It might be awkward at first, but that will pass. If it gets to be too much, can you work different hours?"

"I could try, but it's not easy. I have to be at the shop, too. I can't impose on Amy and Sue like that."

Cassie was right. They had only dated a few times so this should not be so hard. With the other men she had dated, they always seemed to be on the same page. When there wasn't a spark, both people knew it and could part easily. As friends.

But Tim clearly felt something. Which made this all very complicated and exhausting.

"Dinner's ready!" Cassie called into the living room. "We can talk later. You know I'll help you any way I can. You're my best friend and I want you to be happy."

"That's what I want, too."

"Everyone take a seat," Cassie said as the men entered the dining room. "I don't get a chance to cook for this many people very often. I hope you like it." She placed a platter of lasagna and a large bowl of salad down on the table. Kirsten set the garlic bread basket next to them. Wine glasses were filled but no one moved. "It won't kill you, I promise."

Ross dove in first and passed the lasagna to Bear, who sat beside Kade. The salad was passed to Payton, who stared at it as if he'd never seen anything like it before. Instead of taking any he passed the bowl to Kirsten.

"Don't you want any salad?" she asked. "It's really good and good for you, too."

Payton seem skeptical, so she filled his salad plate for him. "Try it. I think you'll be surprised."

He looked up at Bear and then at Ross, who nodded to him. Taking a forkful, he placed it in his mouth and began to chew. The comical expression on his face made Kirsten laugh. She placed a hand on his back. "It's not that bad, is it?"

He shook his head and swallowed. "'Tis good," he said, his voice soft. "I've never eaten this before."

"No salads in Scotland?" Kirsten asked.

"Not where we're from," Ross said.

"What about you, Bear? Do you like it?"

"Aye. 'Tis verra good. I like this, too." He pointed to the lasagna.

"The bread is... like none I've ever tasted," Kade added.

Kirsten was fascinated by the looks of pure pleasure on their faces as they ate. "I guess I take this kind of food for granted. I'm surprised you've never had it before."

None of them answered her as they shoveled the food into their mouths like they hadn't eaten in days.

Cassie wore a huge grin. "Wow! No one has ever enjoyed my food this much."

"I beg to differ, Cassie," Ross said, wiping his mouth with the napkin he lifted from his lap.

"I know you do," she replied with a sweet smile and a wrinkle of her nose.

They were so cute together. Kirsten was happy her friend had found someone special to share her life with.

"We should discuss WinterFest," Cassie said.

"Aye. The lads will help," Ross replied.

"We'll be glad to do our part," Bear added.

"That's great. The inn is booked up and I received the last reservations we can accept for the cottages." Cassie glanced around the table at the others, beaming with pride.

"The ski shop is sponsoring the cross-country race. The course will be set up a day or two before and the numbered bibs will be paid for by our cross-country ski supplier."

"Bands and DJs have been scheduled to play in the barn each night of the festival. Rose is in charge of the food. Walt is in charge of the snow mobile races." Cassie ticked off each item on her fingers.

"Search and rescue and the ski patrol will be on hand in case of any emergencies," Kirsten assured them.

"Is there anything left undone?" Ross asked.

"We need to find people to help with the snowman building contest. We'll need impartial judges. Oh, and also for the ice sculpting."

"That's easy. We've got lots of volunteers to divvy up at each of the events. What about prizes?"

"I'm working on it. If I can get everyone in town to donate an item we should be good."

"Great. We've got it all worked out then."

"It seems we do."

"Yay!" Cassie and Kirsten high-fived each other as the men at the table stared at them as though they were some odd curiosity.

"Most events will take place here in our open fields," Ross explained to Bear and his brothers.

"It's going to be so much fun," Cassie said. "I can hardly wait."

"Let's hope the weather cooperates," Kirsten said, putting a damper on their enthusiasm. At this time of year, it was a given that a storm could appear out of nowhere, dumping several feet of snow in no time. That would make it impossible for people to reach them, putting all their hard work at risk.

"Well, fingers crossed it will," Cassie said. "We've only got another week to wait."

"**G**ood night," Kirsten said, hugging Cassie first and then Ross. "I imagine I'll be seeing all of you again soon," she said to Bear and his brothers.

"Aye. May we walk ye home?" Bear asked.

"Oh, no. That's very nice of you, but I drove."

"We'll be leaving as well," Bear said to Ross and Cassie.

"See you in the morning," Cassie said.

Ross waved to all of them as he closed the door, "Good night."

The three brothers and Kirsten headed down the path to her car. Payton and Kade continued on to their cabin but Bear stayed by her side.

"I hope ye'll forgive us for scaring ye so," Bear said. The sincerity in his voice touched Kirsten.

"As long as you don't do it again," Kirsten teased.

Bear smiled for the first time since they'd met and her heart did a little pitter-pat. She glanced up at him and was aware of how handsome he was as he stood towering above her. He emanated strength and masculinity in a way that was very attractive to her. Her mind went blank and all she could feel was the strange pull drawing her towards him. She mentally shook herself, took a step back and slipped on a sheet of ice by her car door. Bear caught her before she could fall and had her in his arms where she would have been uncharacteristically happy to stay, but this wasn't right. She hardly knew him. "I've got to go." She quickly got into her car and started it up. She gave him a quick wave before driving off.

As Kirsten drove off in one of those strange vehicles that everyone seemed to have, he noticed another one across the road. It roared to life, the lights came on and it took off down the road in the same direction Kirsten had just gone in. He had an uncomfortable feeling as he watched the car disappear from sight. He stood there for a long while and Ross finally joined him.

"Something wrong?" he asked.

"I'm worried about Kirsten," Bear said.

"She'll be fine. She always calls us when she gets home. If she doesn't we'll call her."

"With yer..." he pointed at the pocket he'd seen Ross put his strange device in.

"Aye. 'Tis called a phone. If yer here long enough, ye'll need one."

"I do no' believe I'd ever need a phone." He said the last word like it was a poison he had to spit out.

Ross laughed. "Ye'll change, I've nae doubt."

Bear chuckled. "I've got enough for both of us."

CHAPTER 5

irsten pulled up to her small home cursing the fact that she hadn't left any of the lights on. Just on the outskirts of town, Kirsten loved her little home. She thought about the great view she had of the mountains and how her house smelled like pine trees and snow. Unfortunately, she couldn't appreciate any of that right now because it was so darn dark. She pulled out her phone and used the flashlight app to find her way to the door. She was about to put the key in the lock when a car pulled into her driveway right behind her, its headlights shining right in her eyes and making it impossible for her to see who it was.

"Crap," she said out loud.

"Kirsten," Tim called, as he got out of his car. "I thought I'd make sure you got home from dinner without a problem. You know, you should really leave a light on."

"I know," Kirsten was feeling particularly irritated at his sudden appearance. She unlocked the door.

"Do you mind if I come in?" Tim asked.

"I was going to go right to bed. I'm pretty tired and I've got a busy day ahead of me tomorrow."

"I won't stay long," Tim said, pushing his way past her into the house. "How was dinner?"

"Good," she answered, feeling uncomfortable about Tim's sudden appearance. Had he been following her? "Where'd you come from?"

"I happened to be driving by their place and I noticed you pull out right in front of me."

"I didn't see you." Why would he be on that particular road? There wasn't much beyond the ranch. It wasn't a main thoroughfare so it was rare for cars to head that way unless they were lost.

He shrugged his shoulders.

"Excuse me for a second. I've got to call Cassie and let her know I got home okay."

"Good. I'm glad you do that. I worry about you being alone."

Kirsten couldn't help but grind her teeth at that. He had seen her training records, she was far from helpless. "Why? I'm pretty capable of taking care of myself."

"I know. Of course, you are." He was quick to reassure her. Why did that sound so condescending? She knew they needed to have that conversation but for the life of her she didn't have the energy for it tonight. Tomorrow. Certainly tomorrow she would put an end to this.

She thought she'd made it clear that she was tired and was headed straight to bed, but he wasn't moving any closer to the door. Instead, they stood awkwardly in the living room, staring at each other.

"Were those guys from the avalanche at the house?"

Crap, apparently they were going to talk some more. "They were."

"What were they doing there?"

"They're Ross's cousins."

He scoffed, "More like fools if you ask me."

She was pretty sure Tim had never spoken to them. She could under-stand being angry with them for causing trouble on the mountain, but she had already relayed their apology. It is not as though they were the first people to ever break the rules. "They're actually pretty nice. Ross and Cassie forgot to tell them to stay away from the mountain yesterday."

"Still, you'd think they would've known."

"They're not from around here. They're from Scotland."

Tim was being such a jerk tonight. She didn't even know why they were having this argument. She just wanted him out of here. Kirsten picked up her phone, turned her back on Tim, and punched in Cassie's number. "Hey, it's me. I'm home."

"What's wrong?" Cassie asked.

"Tim's here," Kirsten answered.

"Is everything okay?"

"Yeah. I'll talk to you tomorrow," she hung up, took a deep breath, and turned to Tim. "I don't mean to be rude, but I really need to get some sleep, so if you don't mind." She motioned towards the door. "Thanks for checking up on me."

"Sure. I'll see you tomorrow then." He leaned in for a kiss and Kirsten placed a hand on his chest, stopping him.

"Good night, Tim." Kirsten opened the door, avoiding any further contact with him. She closed and locked the door, peeking through the window to make sure he drove away. The uncomfortable, smothering feeling she'd been getting from him had taken on a whole new level of creepiness. She had to tell him she couldn't be with him, no matter how miserable the conversation would be.

"Surprise," Cassie shouted as she came through the door of the ski shop with Bear. "Someone needs some more appropriate clothing."

Kirsten locked eyes with the handsome Scot and gave him a shy smile. They'd made a connection last night in that brief moment at her car. She wasn't sure what it was, but if those butterflies in her stomach were any indication, she was in trouble. She tore her glance away and focused on Cassie. That should help, but it didn't. She fidgeted with her hair, stammered out something that sounded like, "Sure. I'd be happy to help." She felt like a sixteen year old on her first date.

They walked to the back of the shop where the men's clothing hung on racks from the floor to the ceiling.

"Let's see." Kirsten began going through the racks, unsure of what she was looking for and very aware of the hunk of masculinity standing close behind her. "What did you have in mind?" She glanced over her shoulder to see that Bear seemed as uncomfortable shopping for clothes as she was pretending to be helpful.

"He needs some shirts, sweaters, jeans, socks. You know, pretty much everything."

"Didn't you bring clothes with you?" she asked, feeling somewhat bewildered.

"Nae."

"They lost all their luggage. Can you believe that?" Cassie explained.

"Sure," Kirsten muttered. "Okay, let's start with t-shirts. I've got some on sale back there." She pointed into the furthest corner of the store where she kept all the clearance items. "How many are you thinking?"

"I'd say one for every day of the week. He can wear them under his shirt or sweater."

Kirsten got to work pulling out tees and holding them up to him. His dark hair and eyes looked perfect with just about any color. As they made their choices, she handed them all to Cassie, who seemed to be enjoying herself.

"This reminds me of when Ross first came to town. I had to do the same for him. Remember?"

"I do," Kirsten chuckled. "Okay, now jeans. What size do you wear?"

"I do no' ken," Bear said, looking confused.

"You should measure him. European sizes are different."

"Right." Kirsten got her tape measure and then did a strange dance of moving forward and back, feeling uncomfortable with the close-ness she'd be experiencing. Finally she took a deep breath and wrapped her arms around his waist. A quick glance up told her he was enjoying this. Maybe more than she was. The tape fell out of her hands and she had to try again. Not that she minded. He smelled really good. Very woodsy. Finally she got a measurement and backing away almost tripped over Cassie. "Sorry."

"No worries," Cassie laughed.

She quickly grabbed a few pairs of the right size and sent him into the dressing room to try them on. "OMG," she mouthed to Cassie after he was out of sight. The two of them burst into giggles.

"Use a tape measure much?" Cassie teased.

Bear stood in the small curtained room listening to the women giggling outside and smiling to himself. He held the *jeans* up in front of him trying to decide how exactly to wear them. He knew where his legs went, but he wasn't sure what was the front and what was the back. After a few minutes of turning them this way and that, he put his legs in, pulling them up and securing them around his waist. They were snug, but not uncomfortably so. He threw on one of the shirts Kirsten had chosen for him and looked at himself in the mirror.

"Are you going to come out and show us?" Cassie's voice drifted to him through the curtain.

"Aye," he answered, pulling the curtain open and emerging to find Cassie and Kirsten staring at him. If he wasn't mistaken, Kirsten had gasped. He turned around for them to see and when he looked back they both had a hand over their lips. "Is something wrong?"

"Not a thing," Kirsten said in a breathy whisper.

He went back into the little room and tried on the rest of the clothing, enjoying the delighted expressions on the faces of his audience each time he came out.

"Pick one that you want to wear and when you come out we'll fit you with some socks and boots," Kirsten said.

He did exactly that, expecting sounds of approval, but instead found that when he came out he was greeted by a man who seemed to be waiting for him. Looking past his shoulder, he could see Cassie and

Kirsten near the front of the shop examining boots. He nodded to the man who seemed intent on blocking his passage.

The man seemed to think he was intimidating Bear, but there wasn't much that unnerved him. The fact that this particular man was shorter and slighter than he made him wonder just why he was standing in his way.

"If ye'll excuse me," he said moving closer.

"Stay away from her," he said.

"From who?"

"Kirsten. She's mine. I saw you with her last night. I'm warning you to stay away from her."

Bear took a moment to size this man up. He must have been in the vehicle that followed Kirsten home last night. It was interesting that he hadn't been invited to dinner. Ross and Cassie had been very welcoming to him and his brothers, and they were complete strangers. If this man was important to Kirsten, why wouldn't they include him? Bear had to wonder if it was Kirsten that didn't want him around. He had no right to step in, but he decided to have a bit of fun with the man. "And if I do no'?"

"You'll probably wish you had."

It wouldn't take much for Bear to knock him on his arse, but if Kirsten was this man's woman he could certainly understand his possessiveness. "My apologies, lad. I did no' ken she was taken."

The man moved out of his way and Bear joined Cassie and Kirsten at the boots.

"You look great," Kirsten said.

"Yes, amazing."

"Don't lose that kilt though." Kirsten had a mischievous twinkle in her eye as she spoke.

"He's going to need it for WinterFest. It does need to be cleaned and repaired before then though."

"Are your brothers coming in, too?"

Bear wasn't sure how to answer that. He hadn't expected he'd be here receiving a whole new wardrobe courtesy of Cassie and Ross.

"They will," Cassie said. "I thought having them come in one at a time would be easier for us."

The jealous man appeared at Kirsten's elbow. "Will I see you later?" he asked.

"I don't think so. I'll be here until late."

"When you're done then," he leaned in, kissing a stiff Kirsten on the lips before leveling Bear with what appeared to be a malevolent glare. In fact, it had Bear chuckling to himself as he watched the man stride out the door.

"Is that yer man?" Bear asked.

"No, but he thinks he is." All the laughter had gone out of Kirsten's voice. She seemed unnerved by what had just happened.

"You have to tell him you're not interested, Kirsten," Cassie said.

"I know. I think he followed me home last night after I left your place."

"Really? Is he stalking you?" Cassie asked.

Bear's ears perked up at this. He knew what stalking was. He'd done it himself when hunting wild boar. Was this man hunting Kirsten? That didn't sit well with him. He was no threat to Bear, but how much of a threat was he for Kirsten?

"No. Don't worry about me." Kirsten turned and started straightening the boots on the shelves. "I can take care of myself. I've just got to put my big girl pants on and tell him that this has to stop."

Cassie touched her shoulder and Kirsten's hands stilled. "If you need any help, let me know. Ross will have a talk with him."

Cassie shook her head and shrugged, "It's not that big of a deal. Really. I can handle it."

"Okay."

Without saying a word to the two women, Bear made up his mind that he would become Kirsten's protector. If this Tim did anything at all to harm her, he'd have Bear to answer to. Finding a way to stay close to her would be a challenge.

Adding up the receipts from the past week, Kirsten's head popped up as the bell above the door jingled.

"Hey," Amy said, wiping her feet on the entry mat.

"You're early," Kirsten said.

"Trying to catch that worm." Amy came around the check-out counter to stand beside Kirsten. "How are we doing?"

"Not too bad," Kirsten said. "I think we're going to do really well this year."

"That's good to know. I thought I was going to need to find a third job to supplement my income."

Amy was a worrywart, as Kirsten had come to understand since they'd been in business together these past few years. She was happy to ease her mind. Sue on the other hand didn't seem to have a care in the world. She was definitely a go-with-the-flow kind of gal.

"I saw Tim at the bakery. He asked me to cover for you tonight so he could take you to dinner. I told him I'd be happy to. Anything to advance a little romance in your life."

Kirsten cringed. Tim was really overstepping here. She couldn't blame Amy for trying to help. Her love life had been pretty nonexistent for quite some time now. She wished it wasn't, but there was no way she was going to settle for the first attractive single guy who showed interest in her. Delight wasn't overflowing with men. It was a small town well off the beaten path and living there meant making some sacrifices. It was worth it as far as she was concerned. She'd had her time in the big city. Parties, nights out and the single life in San Francisco were great, but now in her early thirties, Kirsten was happy to be in a place like Delight. She'd learned a lot back then, but now she knew who she was and what she wanted. If Tim had ever had a chance, he was proving to her exactly why he wasn't the man for her.

"You don't look very happy. I thought you'd love the chance to take a night off."

She was going to have to explain this again. If she didn't get her act together she would have explained the break up to the whole town before she got around to telling Tim. "Amy you're such a good friend.

I appreciate that you'd do this for me, I really do. The problem is that I already told Tim I couldn't have dinner with him."

"Wait. You don't want to have dinner with him?" Amy tipped her head, wrinkling her forehead as she obviously tried to understand the situation.

"No. I'm trying to find a way to let him down easy. He's not the one for me."

Amy didn't reply right away, instead she ran her hands through her hair, pulling it back away from her face. It was obvious that she was confused. "I had no idea. I thought you guys were happy together."

How she had gotten that idea was hard to fathom. Kirsten had only gone out with Tim a handful of times and she couldn't remember ever gushing about him to her friends. On the other hand, she did continue to say yes when he asked her out. No wonder Tim thought everything was great between them, even her friends didn't know how she felt. She'd been so busy with work and the festival that it had been a while since she'd had a good talk with her friends. "It's okay. I'll have dinner with him, but I'm telling him we're over. Not that we ever really got started." She needed to have that talk with him, get through the festival and sleep for a few days, then she could refocus on her friendships.

Amy's normally playful attitude turned serious. "If I had known, I would never have agreed with it. I guess all that stuff Tim was telling me wasn't true."

Oh no, he was going around telling people they were a match made in heaven. "Maybe it's true in his head," Kirsten said. The thought of that was disturbing. Had she been giving him mixed signals?

"Well, regardless of your love life, you've been working way too much. This week is going to be crazy with the festival and races to coordinate. Do you think we could possibly afford to hire someone to help out around the store?"

"I think we could. Good idea." Kirsten watched a proud smile spread across Amy's face. "The only problem might be finding some-one, but let's talk to Sue about it and see what we can do."

C assie came back later that afternoon with Payton and then with Kade. Payton had no opinions about the clothes, or much of anything. He was so somber, so quiet. Kade, on the other hand, was a different story. Kirsten had to take care of paper-work and make progress on their never ending to do list so she spread everything out over the display cabinet in the back. She could hear Amy helping Kade pick out some clothes and boots. The two of them were laughing and carrying on like old friends.

Cassie appeared next to her, "Aren't they cute?"

"I don't know who's enjoying this more, them or you," Kirsten said, pointing at the silly grin Cassie was wearing.

"I know. I know. It's just that…"

"What?"

Cassie looked over at Kade and sighed, "The boys have had a rough time of it. Things haven't been going very well for them."

Kirsten knew there had to be more to their story than a simple visit. "Is that why they're here?"

"It is."

"And is it why they don't have clothes?"

"Yes."

"What happened?"

"I'm not allowed to talk about it." She glanced across the room as Amy wrapped an arm around Kade, turning him towards the mirror.

"Gorgeous!" Amy's excited voice carried across the store.

Kade gave her what seemed to be an indulgent smile. He gazed at himself in the mirror, reaching out a hand and running one finger down the glass. Kirsten thought that a bit odd, but Cassie only smiled like a proud mama.

Amy sent Kade back to the dressing room before heading over to speak with Cassie and Kirsten.

"He's adorable. I am absolutely loving this guy." She turned to Cassie. "Anymore like him at home?"

"Yes. Two of them."

"Good, because he's a little young for me."

"You don't say," Cassie teased.

"She has her sights set on men her own age these days," Kirsten said, piling on.

"Hey, that's not fair. I had no idea he was only twenty-one. He lied to me."

Kirsten couldn't stop the fit of giggles that overtook her. Poor Amy had thought she'd found the man of her dreams. It seemed everyone else in town knew how old Drew was, but for some reason it was a complete surprise to Amy. "I'm sorry. We shouldn't make fun of you."

"I really liked him," Amy pouted.

"There's nothing wrong with dating a guy who's younger than you," Cassie chimed in.

"I know. He was a little too young, though, like ten years too young."

Kade joined them at the counter with an armload of clothes and the boots he'd chosen.

"Looks like you've got everything," Cassie said.

"Aye. Thank ye."

"It's nothing. Thank you for helping with the festival."

"What are you going to be doing?" Amy asked.

"Riding through town with me brothers, making the women happy," he beamed.

"Are you serious?" Kirsten said to Cassie.

Cassie straightened her shoulders and gave Kirsten a wink, "Yes. You have to admit that Ross has been really good for business. The Fletcher lads will be too."

"I like the way you think," Amy said, smiling at Kade.

He wrapped an arm around her, kissing her cheek and causing Amy to blush. "Thank ye for all yer help, lass. I've enjoyed *shopping* with ye."

"Any time," Amy said. "I'm here Monday through Friday from noon until we close at six. Weekends are up for grabs."

Kirsten cleared her throat to get Amy's attention. "I don't think he's going to need anything else for quite some time."

"Oh, right." She appeared suitably embarrassed.

"We should get going. Can you add this up for me and put it on my bill?"

"Sure." Kirsten quickly removed the tags from the clothes. "I'll add it all up later."

"Great. Thanks for helping out. Come on, Kade. Let's get you home."

Kirsten walked them to the door. "Talk to you later."

She returned to the counter, collecting the papers she was working on and put them away. She needed to get ready for her date tonight. She'd had such a fun day helping Cassie shop for her lads, but now she had to meet Tim. The rest of the evening was going to be very unpleasant. But afterwards, she could head home for a glass of wine and a hot bath. That thought was going to keep her going for the next few hours. "I'm heading home," she said.

"Okay. See you tomorrow," Amy replied. "Hey, Kirsten, I'm sorry about tonight."

"No worries."

CHAPTER 6

A warm feeling spread through his heart as Bear watched the horses frolicking in the snowy pasture. It reminded him of his life back home. His ma and da bred horses and were known throughout the Highlands to have some of the finest horses in Scotland. They'd tended and cared for many over the years, building a thriving business to pass along to Bear and his brothers. It had been a good life until it all fell apart. They'd lost their land and their horses to the English, who'd shown up unannounced one day and claimed everything. They'd ridden off with all of their horses and given them notice to vacate the property. Payton and Kade had held Bear back knowing that any disobedience would only mean his death at the hands of their enemies. Bear spent many a sleepless night wondering how things had gone so completely wrong. Within the month they'd lost their home, their cattle, and had been forced to a life without food or shelter. They'd spent many a night nearby, hoping against hope that the English would tire of their home and turn it back over to them, but that day never arrived. So, instead, they'd wandered from campsite to campsite, all the while the anger building in them until Bear could stand it no longer. That fateful decision to steal what was rightfully theirs had failed miserably, but had somehow brought them to this place and to these people, but here in this time he was a burden to these strangers. Ross and Cassie had been so kind to them, adding three mouths to feed and purchasing three sets of new clothes. He had no idea how he would repay them, but he would find a way.

His favorite mare, Evie, came to the fence to greet him. Her warm breath releasing clouds of steam into the frigid air. He ran his hand down her neck and then ruffled her forelock before sending her off to join her friends. These horses had a good life. Much better than his family and friends in the year 1747. He'd tried and failed to restore them all to the life they'd enjoyed before Culloden, but with no success. He'd failed his brothers, his clan, and those who'd counted on him to find a solution to their woes.

"Yer deep in thought," Ross said, joining him at the fence.

"Aye."

"Are ye worried about getting back home?"

"I am. I can no' help those who need me from this time and place."

"Nae. Ye cannae, but ye must believe me when I tell ye that yer presence there would do nae good. Ye cannae change what has happened. The course it will take, or took, doesn't bode well for yer success in taking back yer land and possessions. Perhaps 'tis fate that has brought ye here. Ye've no idea how ye got here or how to get back, but perhaps the Old Grey Man has done ye a favor bringing ye here."

They stood quietly for a moment. Bear couldn't shake the helpless feeling he had in the face of all the tragedy he'd left behind. "I believe ye, Ross, but I can no' accept it."

"Ye'll have to for now, my friend. I dinnae ken how we would get ye back there."

"Another avalanche?"

"'Twould be most dangerous. It might work, or ye may end up dead."

"'Tis worth the risk."

"What of Kade and Payton? Is it worth the risk of their lives?"

Bear hadn't thought of that. He'd already put his brothers in more danger than he'd ever imagined possible. He couldn't endanger them yet again for his own selfish purposes. "I'll go alone."

"I'll nae deter ye, but give this time a chance. Ye may find that after a while ye dinnae wish to leave it."

Bear's thoughts went to Kirsten. He didn't wish to leave her. He wanted to spend more time with her, to protect her. There was more there. More to why he didn't want to leave her. More that he didn't wish to examine too closely.

"While I'm here, I'd like to be useful."

"I can understand that."

"I would like to help Kirsten," he said.

Ross's eyebrows shot up. "Kirsten?"

"Aye. I do no' like the man Tim."

Ross continued to eye him with question.

"He has been following her. She does no' like it."

"Then she should tell him so," Ross said. "Ye ken, the women in this time dinnae need men to protect them. A lass like Kirsten, in particular, is quite independent. She willnae appreciate yer protection."

"He told me to stay away from her. Said she was his."

"So yer inclination is to stay closer." Ross looked out over the field, stroking his chin in apparent thought.

"He was here last night, and followed her when she left. I do no' trust him."

That got Ross's attention. "Let me see what I can do."

The two men leaned on the fence watching the horses romp through the snow for several more minutes before turning away.

"If ye wish to be useful, I can use yer help in the barn," Ross said. "Bedding needs to be cleaned and changed." He grabbed a wheelbarrow and pointed to a second for Bear to take. Kade and Payton were doing some repair work to fencing around the property. The heavy snow leaning on the fence posts left several of them broken, taking nearby sections of fence down with them. All three had been sure to help out with any chores they could. They were grateful to Ross and Cassie for their assistance.

Meeting at the restaurant had been Kirsten's idea and had clearly not been Tim's plan. He complained and tried to change her mind for quite some time, but she'd been firm. She could drive herself. When she arrived, she found he was seated and waiting for her. He'd chosen a romantic little French restaurant at one of the big ski resorts near Delight.

Tim rose when he saw her, handing her a beautiful red rose. "You look amazing," he said, his eyes scanning her from head to toe.

"Sorry I'm late." She'd chosen not to look at this as a date and so she hadn't dressed up. She could see Tim silently judging her, but she wasn't about to apologize for that.

"If we'd driven together, you wouldn't be," he said, his obvious irritation hidden by a smile.

"Yeah, well, I told you I had some things to take care of and it was easier for me to meet you here." She could hear the irritation in her voice and she worked to control it. She reminded herself that Tim was a good guy, but this wasn't going to work out and that hopefully they'd remain friends and be able to work together without it being awkward.

"You did say that. What was it you had to do?" he asked.

"There were some things I had to do in Truckee."

"And they were?"

She felt his suspicion. He didn't believe her. Kirsten could have driven up with him, but she *had* gone to Truckee. He didn't need to know that it had been earlier in the afternoon. "We're looking to hire someone to help out in the shop. I was putting help wanted posters up in some of the shops and cafes."

"Does that mean you'll have more free time?" His demeanor changed from suspicious to hopeful in a heartbeat.

"Possibly. We'll see. We have to find someone, train them and then see how they handle the shop."

Their server came bearing appetizers and wine, which she poured into wine glasses placed in front of each of them.

"I took the liberty of ordering for both of us." Tim raised his wine glass. "To the most beautiful woman in the world."

Kirsten did her best to keep from rolling her eyes. Instead she gave him a tentative smile. "That's flattering, but hardly true."

"I'm complimenting you. Accept it." The last was said as an order, which ruffled Kirsten's feathers, but she kept her cool. She had come to dinner with a plan and she had to see it through.

"Okay. Thank you."

He sipped his wine, but Kirsten didn't join him. Instead she placed her glass back on the table. It was now or never. "Tim, there's something I have to say to you."

He lowered his glass and a flicker of something like anger flashed in his eyes.

"This isn't something that is easy for me to say. You are a great guy and I'm flattered that you want to have a relationship with me." She took a deep breath, calming the nerves that were about to erupt, making it difficult for her to say what needed to be said.

"Go on."

"I just don't feel the same way about you. I'm sorry." There, she'd said it. She waited for the explosion she was sure would come, but it didn't happen.

"I see. Is it that Scottish guy who almost got himself killed the other day?"

She couldn't hide her surprise. Where on earth had that come from? "No. There isn't anyone else."

Tim silently nodded his head and then took another sip of wine. "Well, we can at least enjoy dinner together one last time."

"I value your friendship. I want you to know that."

"Good to know."

Their dinner arrived, but Kirsten's appetite never did. She nibbled on what she was sure was a delicious meal, but her taste buds didn't seem to care. Conversation with Tim became stilted and uncomfortable. She tried to keep them focused on work, assignments for the festival days and what the weather patterns looked like for the coming week. All Kirsten wanted to do was go home.

❄

A sense of relief settled in for Kirsten as she drove. Tim's car was right behind her, but that was to be expected. There was only one road back home and they were both headed to Delight. His response to the let down had been muted, making her wonder if she'd been making a bigger deal out of this than she'd needed to. Maybe he wasn't as interested in her as she thought. At any rate, it was over. She could relax and stop worrying about him.

As Kirsten approached her driveway, she noted that Tim was still behind her even though they'd already passed the turnoff for his street. She worried that he was going to pull in behind her, but he only flashed his headlights at her as he drove past. Nothing nefarious there. He only wanted to make sure she got home alright. She got out of her car, happy that she'd remembered to leave the porch light on and easily unlocked her door. She hurried to close and lock it as the phone began to ring.

"Hello?" she answered, bending down to pet her cat Kirby.

"Just checking to see how dinner went," Cassie said. "Amy told me what happened today. Did you finally tell him?"

"I did and he didn't seem too bothered by it."

"Hmmm… interesting."

"I thought so, too. He accepted it without question. Except one. He thought it was because of Bear."

Cassie chuckled. "I could see where he might feel a little threatened by him. He's a handsome man."

"I know." Did she ever. "It's seems like a stretch though. I hardly know Bear. He only arrived in town a few days ago."

"Well, whatever he thinks or thought doesn't matter. You told him how you feel and he accepted it. You won't have to worry about it anymore."

"Right." She couldn't believe what a weight had been lifted from her shoulders. She really should have done it sooner. "Hey, do you know anyone who's looking for a job. We're hiring at the ski shop."

"I don't. Hold on while I ask Ross." The line went quiet while

Kirsten imagined Cassie finding Ross to ask him. "He says he does. He'll bring them by tomorrow when you open."

"Great. Tell him I appreciate it."

"I will."

"If I hire this person, maybe I'll have more time to spend on the winter festival."

"It would be amazing if you could. There's still so much left to do and it's only another week away."

Cassie was the brains behind the whole festival. A year ago, she had gathered everyone together to figure out how to save their town. Ever since, the business owners had banded together to help each other, share resources and ad space, and get creative about how they were going to attract tourists. "Don't worry. It's going to be great. My only hope is that we don't have a snow storm. We need people to be able to get here."

"Fingers crossed. So, getting back to our previous discussion, do you think it'll be hard working with Tim on search and rescue?"

Kirsten felt some of that tension seep back into her shoulders. "I hope not. We'll see. I won't know for sure until it happens. I'm telling you though, he acted like it was no big deal."

"I'm relieved to hear it. The last thing you need is someone stalking you."

"Yeah. I'm embarrassed to say I might have overreacted a bit."

"I don't think so. You can never be too careful."

"Very true."

"Well, I for one am happy to know you finally told him."

"Me, too."

"I've got to go. Ross is in the kitchen!"

Kirsten laughed. "Bye." Ross was, according to Cassie, always trying to cook some old Scottish recipe and he had no idea what he was doing. She could just picture Cassie rushing to help him so he wouldn't burn their house down. She was incredibly happy for Cassie. She and Ross were an adorable couple. A perfect match. Maybe someday she'd be that lucky.

Kirsten had been searching for Mr. Right for some time now.

She'd thought she might find him in San Francisco, but that never happened. The tech world had changed the dynamics in the city and she hadn't been sorry to leave it all behind. Coming home to Delight was the last thing she would have ever imagined she'd want to do when she was in high school. She'd been in a hurry to get out of here, not fully appreciating it for the wonderful place that it was. Spending so many years away in a place where she never felt one hundred percent comfortable, she'd been homesick. Something she couldn't admit to herself or to anyone else. It took a trip back here to help her parents pack up for their move to Reno for her to realize that home is where the heart is and her heart was definitely in Delight. She loved all three of her jobs, the clean fresh air, lack of traffic and the fact that she was surrounded by family. Not blood relatives, but the people of Delight. They were her family and while it could be a bit much that they all knew every last detail of her love life, she wouldn't have it any other way. This was her home and this is where she planned to stay. If Mr. Right was out there, he was going to have to find her here in Delight and be willing to stay.

"This was easier than I thought it would be," Ross said as they approached the ski shop. "The festival is coming up, so Kirsten should have plenty for ye to do."

Bear opened the door leading into the shop and was greeted by Kirsten who, head down, didn't even realize who he was.

"Welcome to the shop, if I can help you with anything let me know." She continued staring at some papers in her hands.

"Good day to ye, lass," Ross said.

Her head popped up, "Ross!" Her eyes flicked from Ross to Bear. "Hi," she said with a small wave. "Cassie said you were bringing someone to help in the shop."

"And I have." He glanced at Bear.

"Oh..." She seemed at a loss for words, but eventually spoke again.

"It's nice of you to think of me and to want to help, but I really don't think Bear is the right person for the job."

Bear tipped his head, silently questioning her reasoning.

"Don't get me wrong. You're a great guy and, like I said, I appreciate you wanting to help. It's just that you don't know a thing about retail."

"Retail?" He repeated the word unsure of its meaning.

Ross hurried to is aid. "Kirsten, he's volunteering his time. He can do anything ye need."

Bear noted the skepticism on Kirsten's face.

"Ye'll be needing help with the festival. He can carry boxes and help with the heavy work. In the meantime, ye can continue to search for someone else who knows retail, as ye say."

The two men watched her mulling this over in her head. Bear was quite sure she was going to send them on their way and then he'd have to find another way to stay close enough to protect her.

"Alright. I guess I really could use someone in the stock room. Of course, the festival will be the most important job."

"Good. I'll leave him here with ye then," Ross said, backing towards the door. "Cassie wanted me to tell ye that she has the signs for the cross-country race. Do ye think ye can pick them up from the house tonight?"

"Sure. No problem."

"Aye, then ye can drive Bear home when yer work is done." He quickly darted out the door before Kirsten could object, which from the look of her, Bear thought was more than possible.

Kirsten looked him up and down, which Bear found rather amusing. Even more so when she realized what she'd been doing and looked up at his face. A slow pink hue crept over her and she quickly looked away.

"Come with me," she said, walking towards the back of the store. "This is the stock room. It needs a major clean up and reorganization." The large room was piled high with boxes. So much so, that Bear wondered how they'd managed to stack them so high. Shelving lined the walls and a few tables were covered with piles of clothing. Bear listened carefully as she told him what needed to be done. It was important to him. He wanted to help her and he also wanted to make sure Tim didn't bother her ever again. "When you're done, we'll work on the festival." Kirsten headed back to the shop, but turned to him one more time before leaving. "Thank you for volunteering. It means a lot to me and to Delight."

Bear turned to the task at hand. He stacked unopened boxes, clearing a path to the back door and put the clothing laying around in piles everywhere onto hangers as Kirsten had showed him. He grouped them together by item and by color, and also by size. Kirsten showed him wear to look for the letters, which he again grouped together. Once he had everything in place, he swept the floor, threw away any trash he found and was just about to go in search of Kirsten when another woman entered the room.

"Hi. You must be Bear. I'm Sue, Kirsten's business partner." She held out her hand to him and he awkwardly took it, unsure of what to do with it. "Nice to meet you."

"And ye," he replied.

"Wow! You did a great job. Thanks so much for your help." He watched as Sue made her way around the stock room. "I can actually walk around here without tripping over stuff." Her broad grin was infectious and Bear found himself smiling back. "Now, let's go see if we can find something for you to do in the shop." Sue threaded her arm through his and walked him back out front where Kirsten's face wore a curious expression.

"You have to go see the stock room, Kirsten. It's immaculate and so organized. Sue had her arm through Bear's and appeared to be quite cozy with him. For some reason Kirsten couldn't put a finger on, this rankled her. "I thought we could use him out here with us. The ladies coming in will love him, just like they love Ross at the bookstore."

"I don't know—"

"What's to know? We'll give him some on the job training. It'll be great. You'll see."

She was about to answer when the door opened and Tim walked through. She closed her eyes and let out a giant sigh, which caught everyone's attention.

"Are you okay?" Sue asked.

"Fine. Just tired I guess."

Bear untangled himself from Sue and moved closer to Kirsten.

"Well, you sure get around, don't you?" Tim said to him.

What did he mean by that, Kirsten wondered? And why was he here? She was pretty sure he understood her last night when she'd told him she wasn't interested in seeing him.

"Am I missing something?" Sue asked, glancing from Kirsten to Bear to Tim.

"Not a thing," Tim said. "I needed some new ski clothes and this is the only store in town that carries what I need. That's not a problem is it?" He gazed at Kirsten, who didn't like the edge she heard in his voice.

"Sue can help you," Kirsten said.

Sue raised an eyebrow in her direction, but didn't question her out loud. "Bear, why don't you come with. We'll consider it training."

Bear followed along behind them, leaving Kirsten alone at the register wondering exactly what Tim was up to.

After a few minutes of pretending to look over receipts, Kirsten wandered closer to Sue, Bear and Tim, hiding behind a large display of skis and poles. She straightened and rearranged some hangers, all the while eavesdropping on their conversations.

"Do you have this one in another color?" Tim held up a green puffy jacket.

"I'll check." Sue walked away towards the stock room leaving the two men eyeing each other territorially.

"I told you to stay away from her." Tim's clipped tone took Kirsten by surprise.

"The lass needed help here at her store." Bear kept his voice calm.

73

"Tell her you can't work here after today." Tim's aggressive behavior was scaring her, but Bear seemed to have it under control.

"Why would I do that?" Bear's relaxed posture showed no sign that Tim was affecting him in any way.

"Because if you don't, you'll regret it," Tim snarled.

"There's that word regret again. I surely will no' regret…"

"I have it in navy." Sue returned and presented him with her find.

"Nah. Never mind." He barely looked at it. As he turned to leave, he cast a baleful glare in Bear's direction and received a knowing smile and a wink for his effort.

Kirsten couldn't believe what she'd just seen. Tim had threatened Bear, and apparently not for the first time. He still wanted her. She'd never been in this type of situation before and she wasn't quite sure what to do.

"Soooooo… that was strange," Sue said, joining her as she absently fingered the clothing she stood beside. "What is going on with him?"

Good gracious, if they couldn't even manage a simple clothing purchase, how were they going to work together for hours on end. "I told him last night that it was over."

Sue laughed and rolled her eyes, "Well, that explains it. Bear could you hang that blue jacket up with the green one?"

"I was surprised to see him here today," Kirsten said, feeling incredibly vulnerable.

"Maybe he thought it wouldn't be weird for him to come in to shop. But he was wrong. I guess from now on he'll be buying his clothes somewhere else. No great loss. So he got his little man feelings hurt, that's on him not you. He'll get over it."

Sue didn't seem to be too bothered by it all, but why would she? She wasn't the one who'd been dating him and she'd missed the inter-action between him and Bear.

"Bear, could I speak with you a minute?"

She headed back to the stock room and he followed along behind her.

"I overheard your conversation with Tim."

"Aye." He didn't seem any more bothered by the interaction than Sue did.

"What did he mean about you staying away from me?"

Bear hesitated. "He told me the other day when I was here that he did no' want me near ye. He said ye were his."

She could feel the anger bubbling up inside of her. What an ass. He had not only been spreading his version of their relationship to her friends, but apparently anyone in town was fair game. "I'm so sorry. I don't know what's gotten into him. He was never like this before."

"He feels threatened."

"He shouldn't. I told him I didn't want to see him anymore. It's not like we were married or something. He doesn't own me." She kicked a box out of the way, stubbing her toe and yelping in pain. She grabbed onto a nearby workbench to steady herself.

Bear was at her side in an instant, taking her into his arms and surrounding her with his strength. Where she'd felt exposed and threatened before, she now felt safe in his embrace. "I'll protect ye, lass. Have nae fear. He will no' harm ye. Ye can be sure of it."

CHAPTER 7

*B*ear was enjoying the feel of Kirsten in his arms. It had been a long time since the warmth of a woman so close to his heart had touched him so deeply. He wanted to continue holding her, but Kirsten pushed herself away.

"I'm fine. I was shocked is all." She brushed her hair back from her face, revealing eyes the color of the sky on a bright, sunny day and a soft sensual mouth the color of soft, pink roses.

"I mean to protect ye, lass." Bear stated.

"I'm pretty sure I can take care of myself."

He wanted to tell her that she couldn't. That she needed him, but he could see she was a proud lass and he had learned from his conversation with Ross, the women of this time were quite used to doing things for themselves. He wouldn't insult her by arguing otherwise. "I've nae doubt that ye can, but I do no' trust him."

"He wouldn't hurt me." The words sounded confident, but there was something in her eyes, an uncertainty that he had not seen in her before.

Bear nodded at her. She wanted to believe Tim wasn't dangerous and Bear didn't have anything to say that could change her mind so he let it drop. But he would need to stay close. "Alright. I'm here if ye need me." He glanced around the store and then back to Kirsten. "What do I do now?"

"How about lunch? My treat."

Food was always welcome, so he nodded and they headed to the front of the store,

"Sue, we're going to lunch." Kirsten called out.

"Okay," Sue called from the across the store.

Kirsten grabbed her jacket and tossed Bear his.

"We'll go to the bakery. Rose will be thrilled to see you."

"Rose, the lass who makes the scones?"

"Yes. She makes great sandwiches, too. You'll see."

She led the way out the door and he followed, closing it after them. The air was sharp, biting at his skin as they walked. He would have liked to pull Kirsten closer for warmth and for other selfish reasons, but she seemed to be in quite a hurry. They crossed the street, only having to wait for one car to pass. Bear found himself the recipient of smiles and waves from many of the people Ross had introduced him to the other day and he was happy to return their greetings.

Kirsten moved ahead of him on the narrow sidewalk. Snow piled on the sides left room for only one to pass. She smiled back at him and his heart melted. "I'm so hungry." she said, reaching for the door of the bakery. "And cold."

The bakery was warm and smelled of sweets. It was a comforting scent. The aroma brought Bear back to his mother's kitchen. The smell of freshly baked bread warm with butter. His mouth began to water at the memory.

"Kirsten! Bear! It's so good to see you both."

"Hi, Rose!"

"Good day to ye," Bear said.

"I like that. Good day!" Rose said in return. "I've just taken some croissants out of the oven. Can I make you a sandwich?"

"Sounds good," Kirsten said. "What kind are you making today."

"Either ham and cheese or turkey with cranberry aioli."

"Touch choice." She looked to Bear, but he wasn't sure what to say.

"Why not get one of each and you can share?"

"How does that sound, Bear?"

That was a much easier question, "Good."

"If you want more, we can always order another." Kirsten turned to Rose and said, "We'll take one of each."

"Drinks?"

"I'll take tea," Kirsten said.

"Black, green or herbal?" Rose asked.

Bear didn't know there were so many kinds of tea. He was mulling this over in his head and didn't notice that Rose was waiting for a reply.

"I'm having English breakfast," Kirsten told him.

He didn't like the sound of that. "Do ye have something Scottish?"

"I think I do. Let me check. I'll be back in a bit, make yourselves comfortable."

Kirsten removed her jacket and Bear did the same. They took a seat at a small, wooden table. It was intimate, much smaller than those they'd had in the village tavern at home. He was fascinated by the large glass window across the entire front of the store. People walking by on the sidewalk looked in, some smiling and waving to those inside. Rose's beautiful baked goods filled cases that created a divider between the tables and a wall of more baked goods and other things. A single door was open to the back of the bakery.

"It's nice and warm in here," Kirsten said. "Tell me about yourself. All I know about you is that you're Ross's cousin and that you and your brothers are from Scotland."

"What would ye like to know?" He had to tread carefully here. He didn't want to say anything that would raise suspicion about who they were.

"Where in Scotland are you from?"

"The Highlands." He decided it would be best to keep his answers short.

"Is it just you and your brothers or do you have other siblings?"

"'Tis just us. This bakery reminds me of home."

"How so?"

"The warmth. The aroma of fresh baked bread. It brings me back there."

"They say the sense of smell is closely linked with our memories. I know for me, certain smells remind me of Christmas or the beach. If I smell roses, it takes me right back to my grandmother's garden."

"'Tis the way of it." It was true. He'd never really given it much thought before this very moment.

Rose came back with two steaming mugs of tea, which she placed in front of them. "You're in luck, Bear. I have a very special Highland brew just for you."

"Thank ye, Rose." The people he'd met so far in Delight, with the exception of Tim, were kind and generous. Again he thought of home. Delight reminded him of his village before it was destroyed by the English. He cleared his throat as he tried to clear the memories of the death and destruction he'd seen. His friends and neighbors leaving him and his brothers one-by-one for a hopefully better life. His brother Payton's devastation at the loss of his wife and bairn from an illness that swept their small burg.

"Are you okay?" Kirsten asked. "You seem to have drifted off somewhere."

"Some memories are best left forgotten," he said.

Kirsten tipped her head, sadness filling her eyes. He could feel her empathy reaching out to him as her hand touched his. "I'm so sorry. I don't know what's made you sad, but I'm here for you if you ever want to talk about it."

He forced a smile. How could he drag her into his sorrow? "Thank ye." It meant more to him than he could express that this woman he barely knew somehow could feel his pain and she wanted to help. He hoped she knew how much it meant to him, because the words couldn't pass his lips.

"Rose those look delicious," Kirsten said as Rose placed their food on the table.

"I cut them in half and gave you one of each," she said. "Save room for dessert. I've got something special I've been working on for you to try. It's something I'm making for the festival." She placed a hand on Bear's shoulder, giving it a slight squeeze before leaving them.

"Oh, this is delicious," Kirsten said. "I love the cranberry aioli!" She called towards the kitchen.

"Happy to hear it," Rose called back.

"What do you think?" Kirsten asked.

He had a mouth full of food and was unable to answer her. She beamed a smile across the table to him.

"Never mind. I can see how much you're enjoying it."

"What are these?" he asked when he was finally able to speak. He held up a thin crunchy piece of food.

"Potato chips." She looked at him with surprise. "You've never had chips before?"

"Nae." He knew what potatoes were, but he'd never seen them like this. It was crunchy and salty. He decided he needed another.

Kirsten laughed at him and the sound was even better than potato chips. "Your village must be out in the middle of nowhere," she said.

"'Tis."

"How far is the nearest store?"

Finally, a question he could answer easily. "We had one right on our property. The lads and I dug it out. It took a good deal of time, but when it was finished, we had a good space to store our food."

Confusion clouded her face, "Oh, I'm sorry. I used the wrong word. I meant a shop. Like this one."

He chuckled. "I see. 'Twould be far. It could be a million miles away and I would no' ken it."

"Hmmm... I'm trying to imagine what it would be like to live somewhere without shopping. I don't think I could do it."

"'Tis nae so hard."

"For you," she laughed. "If I don't get down the mountain to a mall every now and again, I go into withdrawal."

He tried not to appear confused. He had no idea what a mall was, but based on their conversation, he assumed it was a place to shop.

"What do ye buy at this mall?"

"Mostly clothes and shoes. Sometimes make up or jewelry. Things for my house. You know—stuff."

He didn't know, but he nodded his head and kept eating. If his mouth was full he wouldn't have to answer anymore questions.

"What do you do for fun where you're from?" she asked.

He swallowed his food before answering. "My brothers and I like to race with our horses. We wager on who will be the fastest. I usually win," he proudly stated. "We've much work to do, but there are times when we go down to the creek and spend some quiet time fishing. Sometimes we go off to hunt and sleep out under the stars."

"You could do all of those things here in Delight when the weather warms. I love to go fishing and camping. There are some really beautiful places here in the Sierra."

"Ye fish?" he asked.

"I do. If I catch any, I let them go."

"Why? Do ye no' eat them?" This was puzzling to him. Why would someone take the time to fish and then not eat what they caught.

"I fish for fun. I'm not interested in cleaning and cooking the fish. That's what restaurants are for," she laughed.

He loved the sound of her laughter. "Perhaps I will take ye fishing if I'm still here in the spring. I'll clean and cook the fish for ye."

"I'd like that," she said, lowering her eyes to look at her plate.

He could imagine spending more time with her camping out under the stars. The possibility of it warmed his heart.

Lunch was turning out to be one of Kirsten's best ideas. She was sitting across from a totally hot Highlander who, from the looks of it, must have been starving.

"Rose, I think your sandwiches were a success," she said as Rose came by to check in on them.

"Do you want another?" she asked Bear.

"Which did you like best?" Kirsten asked him.

"The turkey," he said, a huge smile on his face.

"Another turkey," Kirsten said.

"On the way." Rose headed back to the kitchen.

There were so many things Kirsten wanted to know about Bear, but he was the strong silent type, it seemed. She'd asked him some questions and watched as he'd retreated inside of himself, obviously remembering things that were too upsetting to share. *Maybe once I know him better he'll open up to me,* she thought. In the meantime, she'd do her best to keep things on the light side. Their conversation about fishing and camping seemed to bring him out of his shell. She'd have to remember that.

Rose brought another sandwich and she brought Kirsten a giant sugar cookie which had been decorated with the town name along with beautiful pine trees covered in snow.

"Rose! This is amazing!" Kirsten couldn't believe how beautiful it was. "People are going to love these cookies."

"Do you really like it?"

"Yes! Unbelievable. What do you think, Bear?"

He gazed at the cookie with wonder in his eyes before turning to Rose. "Yer an artist and a baker!"

"Oh, I don't know about that," she replied, a bit of pink tinging her cheeks.

"He's right! This is so beautiful that I don't want to eat it."

"Well, cookies are for eating. Besides, I'm planning on making dozens more."

"Will you share it with me, Bear?" she asked.

"No sharing. He can have his own," Rose teased, before turning to Bear. "Would you or your brothers be interested in helping with the cookies?"

"I'm helping Kirsten at her shop, but Kade might be able to help. I'll ask him when I see him later." This would be a good job for him. He was much improved but still looked a little unbalanced. Bear wanted to be sure he had a job that kept him inside.

"Oh, good. I'm going to need help with production." Rose wandered back towards the kitchen muttering something about putting the cookies on the website.

"The festival is going to be so much fun. It's the first and if it goes well, it will be an annual event. Cassie's been working so hard to put Delight on the map."

"'Tis no' on the map?"

Kirsten couldn't help but laugh. "Of course it is, I mean we want people to know we're here so that they'll come stay at our inn, eat in our restaurants and shop in our stores. Last year at this time, we weren't sure any of the town's businesses would survive, but Cassie and Ross saved us."

Bear's face reflected his interest in what Kirsten was saying. She liked that. The men she'd known over the years hadn't always been willing to listen or been interested in the things she had to say.

"I'm glad Delight was saved. If it had no' been, I do no' know where I'd be right now."

"Probably in the same place, but with a lot of very unhappy people."

"Ye *are* a cheer filled group," Bear said, his eyes twinkling with humor.

She liked Bear. In fact, she liked him a lot. "How long are you and your brothers in town for?"

Bear shifted in his chair, looking uncomfortable. "That remains to be seen. We'd like to return home, but that may be difficult."

"Why would it be difficult? Are you having trouble booking a flight or something."

He seemed puzzled by her question.

"Or is it because you want to stay?"

"'Tis a lovely place and everyone has been kind. But... 'tis no' home."

"You don't want to talk about it, do you? Here I am asking questions that are none of my business. Sorry. At least you'll be here for the festival." She tried not to sound too disappointed. It figured that a guy finally arrived in Delight that she found attractive, interesting and who seemed to be a genuinely good person, but he probably wasn't staying. That was the kind of luck Kirsten expected when it came to men—bad.

They finished their lunch and Rose sent them off with two baskets of cookies. One to share with the girls at the ski shop and one for Bear to bring home to Cassie, Ross and his brothers.

Bear was a big help in the shop that afternoon. Kirsten couldn't believe how much they'd managed to get done. Things that had been on their to do list for a while were all checked off.

"We've cleared the to do list. I never thought that would happen," Sue said.

"I guess we really did need some extra help around here," Kirsten answered. "Amy will be in to relieve you in a bit, I'm going to drive Bear home and I'll see you tomorrow."

"Good night," Sue said, walking them to the door.

"Will she be alright there by herself?" Bear asked as they got into her car.

"Sue? She's a black belt in Tae Kwon Do. No one's going to mess with her." Bear was wearing that same puzzled expression again, but she figured he'd ask if he really had a question.

"What about ye? How will ye stay safe?" he asked. She could hear the concern in his voice and it touched her heart, but she was a woman who was very capable of taking care of herself. She'd been doing it for years.

"I know a thing or two about being safe. You really don't have to worry about me." He didn't seem convinced. "You know I'm part of the search and rescue crew here in Delight and I'm on the ski patrol. If I'm capable of rescuing other people, I'm capable of rescuing myself."

They'd reached her car and Kirsten unlocked the door before getting in the driver's side. Bear got in the car, scanning it from top to bottom, his eyes darting from the front seat to the back. It was almost like he was unfamiliar with cars, but she knew that couldn't be true. He'd come into town earlier with Ross in Cassie's truck. He fumbled with the seatbelt before clicking it into place. He had an old fashioned quality about him that she liked.

The road to Ross and Cassie's place was pretty much deserted and the two of them drove the road through the trees in a comfortable silence. The sky was dark now and the only lights on the road came from her car. A light sprinkling of snow began to fall, causing Kirsten to let out a deep sigh.

"Is something wrong?" Bear asked.

"Not really." She paused for a minute, collecting her thoughts. "The snow. It's a blessing and a curse."

"What do ye mean?"

"We need the snow to have a successful ski season, but when it snows a lot it makes it hard for people to get up here. Not that they won't give it a try. This stuff's pretty light. Hopefully it won't dump too much snow on us right before the festival." She could feel his eyes on her, so she took a quick glance in his direction. He was watching her, but not in a creepy way like Tim. His gaze warmed her, sent her heart racing and caused her belly to do flip flops. It was an all together pleasurable sensation.

Kirsten pulled into the driveway of what had once been an old run down ranch. Since Cassie purchased it last year, it had regained its original beauty while keeping its charming, rustic looks. "We're here," she announced and then was immediately embarrassed at how dumb that sounded. Of course they were here, Bear didn't need her to tell him. He could see for himself. He got out of the door without a word and she watched as he passed in front of the car and walked up to her door. He opened it and gave her his hand, which she readily took as he helped her out.

"Thank you," she said, gazing up into deep, dark eyes that softened as she got closer. She placed a hand on his chest as he cupped her face with his hands. He was going to kiss her. She licked her lips in anticipation.

"Hey you two, come in out of the cold," Cassie shouted from the doorway.

Bear reluctantly removed his hands, and turned towards the porch, holding out a hand and directing her in front of him. Kirsten took a deep breath, calming herself and willing her body to stop tingling from her brush with an almost kiss from Bear Fletcher.

"You're just in time for dinner," Cassie said, holding the door open for them.

"Oh, I don't know if I can stay," Kirsten protested.

"Why not? What other plans have you got for the night?"

Cassie had her there. The only thing waiting for her at home was her cat and like most cats, he didn't really need her. He'd be fine for another couple of hours. "Alright. You convinced me."

"Good. I made a nice minestrone soup. My mother's Italian roots have been showing up in my cooking lately. I hope you like it."

"It smells delicious," Kirsten said as the aroma from the soup and freshly baked bread wafted across the room.

"Brother, join us!" Kade, the youngest brother was seated near the fireplace with Payton and Ross. "Ross has some fine whisky to share with us."

"How was your first day of work?" Cassie asked.

"I was happy to help Kirsten," Bear said.

"That's a very diplomatic answer. What did you really think?"

He laughed at her, "I think 'twas hardly work."

"He was a big help. The store hasn't looked that organized in ages." She beamed at Bear, who's lopsided grin in return was adorable. "Tomorrow we're going to set the course for the cross-country ski race and for the snowshoe race."

"Ye've a spot picked out then?" Ross asked.

"I think we should keep it close to the ranch, since it is going to be the central location for everything. There's a pretty decent path on the edge of your property. It should be perfect for our purposes."

"I ken the one," Ross said. "Yer right."

Ross poured Bear some whisky.

"Hey, what about me?" Kirsten teased.

Ross seemed surprised, but sent an unspoken message to Cassie.

"Here's a glass," Cassie said as she handed it to her.

Ross filled her glass about halfway.

"Thank you. I'd like to make a toast." She raised her glass. "Here's to a successful WinterFest, to old friends and to new friends." They all clinked glasses and drank.

Kirsten almost forgot that Rose needed help at the bakery. She had the basket of cookies at her side and hadn't yet given them to Cassie.

"Rose sent a little present for you. She made them especially for the festival."

Cassie took the basket from her and uncovering the cookies, she gasped. "These are unbelievable! She's amazing!"

"They taste pretty darn good, too. Don't they Bear?"

"Aye. That they do. Kade, they need some help at the bakery and Rose wondered if ye'd like a job."

Kade looked over the cookies with eyes like saucers. "Do ye think I could help her? I'm no' a baker."

"She probably needs someone to take over some of the other duties so she can focus on the cookies. Don't worry, Rose will show you what to do."

"Aye, then. I'll do it." Kade beamed from ear to ear. "Spending the day surrounded by food sounds like the best job there is."

"What of ye, Payton?" Bear asked.

Payton tipped his head in question.

"Would ye like a job?"

"I'm happy here, helping Ross and Cassie."

"That *is* a pretty big job," Cassie said.

"Aye. He works hard." Ross clapped Payton on the back.

Kirsten observed the brothers. Of the three, Payton seemed to be the quietest. It wasn't that Bear was a big talker, but Payton seemed emotionally drained, like something had happened in his life that he was still dealing with. She'd have to remember to ask Bear about it.

"Shall we sit down to eat?" Cassie asked.

She didn't need to wait for an answer. The men were up and at the table in no time. Cassie followed along with Kirsten.

The meal was eaten and quiet conversation exchanged among the group.

"I've never had soup like this," Kade said. "When we would go hunting together, Bear was always the cook and he was verra bad at it." This prompted everyone to laugh.

"So, Bear when you told me you'd take me fishing and clean and cook the fish, you omitted the part about not being a very good cook. I might have to rethink that," Kirsten teased.

"I can cook fish," he stubbornly stated.

"Aye. He can. I forgot about that," Kade said.

"Kirsten do you remember that camping trip the two of us took a few years back?" Cassie asked.

"I'm not sure I like where this is going, but yes, of course I do," Kirsten replied.

"Neither one of us was used to cooking over a campfire and we burned absolutely everything we tried to cook. And when I say burned, I mean it was like eating a piece of charcoal. We even burned the s'mores and that's not an easy thing to do."

"I don't know where we went wrong there," Kirsten laughed.

"What are s'mores?" Kade asked.

"They're yummy treats made with graham crackers, chocolate and marshmallows. The marshmallows are the only thing you're supposed to heat in the campfire, but we put everything in a pan and tried to do it that way. What a mess!"

The stories continued with good natured ribbing all around and Kirsten felt a sense of family she hadn't had in a long time.

CHAPTER 8

*P*ulling into her driveway, Kirsten was immediately aware something was wrong. Her cat, Kirby, was sitting smack in the middle of the yard. Her heart immediately jumped to her throat. Kirby was an indoor cat. Had she left the door open all day? Kirsten racked her brain trying to remember her morning routine, but she was sure she'd closed and locked her door. As she pulled in closer, her headlights showed her front door wide open. In the summer months, bears were a problem, breaking into some cabins, but her door was pretty bear proof and it was winter when the bears weren't active at this time of year.

She sat in her car for a minute before deciding to call the police on her cell. She explained her concern and they told her to stay where she was and they'd be there as fast as possible.

"Kirby," she called to her cat, who sauntered over to her open car door. Once he was inside, she closed and locked the door. She shivered and held Kirby close. "Looks like you had an adventure today," she said. When she thought of all the things that could have possibly happened to him, she nearly wept. She picked up her phone again and called Cassie.

"Someone broke into my house," she said, having a hard time believing it.

"What?"

"I just got home and my front door is wide open. Kirby was outside."

"Oh, no. We're on our way."

"It's okay. The police will be here in a few minutes."

"I don't care. I'm coming over."

Cassie hung up before Kirsten could say another word. Lights flashed in her rearview mirror as Sheriff Stengahl pulled in behind her. He exited his car and Kirsten rolled down her window.

"Stay here," he said, drawing his gun and approaching her front door. "This is the police. Come out with your hands up." He waited a few minutes before repeating his order. When no one appeared, he entered, turning on the lights and heading from room to room. A short time later he exited and came back to her car. "No one's there. It looks like someone rummaged through your stuff."

Another car pulled into the driveway behind the police car.

"Hey, Tim."

"Sheriff," Tim said. "I was driving by and saw your car. Is everything alright?"

Kirsten got out of the car, still cradling Kirby.

"Kirsten, my God, are you okay?" He pulled her into his arms and crushed her to him. Kirby let out a yowl and he released her. She would have to remember to give Kirby a treat later.

"I'm fine. I arrived home to find my cat outside and my front door open." She couldn't believe someone would do that.

"It's a rare day when something like this happens in Delight," Sheriff Stengahl said. "I could count on one hand the number of times I've had a call like this over the last ten years. It's usually someone passing through town. Take a look around and see if anything's missing. We can file a police report for your insurance company."

"Thanks. I'll do that."

"I'll stay with her, Sheriff. I don't want her to be here alone."

That was the last thing she wanted. "You don't need to," Kirsten protested. "The sheriff already checked the house. There's no one here."

"I doubt they'll be back," Sheriff Stengahl assured him.

"Still, I don't like it. You shouldn't be alone," Tim insisted.

Cassie's truck pulled into the driveway, squeezing past Tim's car and the patrol car to come to a stop next to her. Ross, Cassie and Bear jumped out.

"Are you okay?" Cassie asked, placing a comforting arm around Kirsten's shoulders.

"I'm fine. I'm more upset about Kirby than anything they might have taken from my house. I have no idea how long he was outside for."

The sheriff went back inside while the others stood around in the driveway.

"Kirsten has decided I should stay here with her," Tim said, directing his gaze at Bear.

"No. I didn't, Tim." How dare he? She didn't even try to hide her irritation. "I told you I'm fine. You can go now."

"I don't think so. You're in shock."

What was he up to? She wasn't in shock. If anything, she was angry at this whole situation. Not to mention annoyed at his terrible timing. If only she had stayed at Cassie's an hour longer, he would have driven right past and never seen the police car.

"We'll stay here with her, Tim. No need to worry about her. I can spend the night here if you like," Cassie said.

"That would be great," Kirsten answered. Maybe that would get Tim to leave her alone. "Tim, thank you for stopping, but I'm going to be alright. I've got Cassie here with me."

The expression on his face was hard to read, but he didn't seem happy. "Alright. I'll be home if you need me. Please don't hesitate to call if there's anything I can do."

"I will," she replied.

They all watched as he walked back up the driveway to his car and departed.

Kirsten let out a sigh of relief, "I wasn't sure he was going to leave."

"That's why I offered to stay. Although I don't know how much good I'd do if the person who broke in came back."

"I can stay with ye," Bear offered.

"Are you sure?" Kirsten asked, allowing herself to feel vulnerable for the first time now that Tim was gone. She hadn't wanted him to see her like this or he'd never have left. It was best that Tim walked away thinking that none of this had bothered her and she wasn't in the least bit afraid to stay here tonight.

"Aye."

"Alright. I'll take you up on that." She didn't have to examine her feelings about having an overnight guest. There was no question she didn't want Tim to stay, but Bear was another story altogether.

Sheriff Stengahl came out of the house again. "I double checked everything, made some notes and if you've got someone to stay here with you tonight, I think you'll be fine."

"Thanks. I appreciate you coming so quickly. Bear's going to stay with me."

"I don't believe I've had the pleasure," the sheriff said, holding out a hand to Bear. "Sheriff Stengahl."

"Bear Fletcher." Bear shook the proffered hand.

"'Tis my cousin," Ross said.

"Here from Scotland, I'm guessing."

"Aye. With my two brothers."

"Well, I'll leave you then. If you need me at any time during the night, don't hesitate to pick up the phone. You can stop by the station tomorrow with a list of anything that was stolen."

"Thanks, Sheriff."

"Good night, folks."

He left them and Kirsten turned towards her house. She clutched Kirby a little tighter and squared her shoulders, then entered her house with the others following behind. Her living room looked like a tornado hit it. Books and photos were on the ground, all the couch cushions were thrown around, everything was tossed all over the place. Strangely, her television was hanging on the wall and untouched. Maybe they hadn't brought tools to remove it.

"What a mess," Cassie said.

"Yer door's broken," Ross noted as he tried to close it.

"Great. Just great."

"I've got some tools in the back of the truck. I believe Bear and I can fix it for ye." With confident strides, they disappeared outside.

"Where did you find him?" Kirsten asked.

"I didn't. He found me," Cassie replied. There was something so peaceful in her voice, a surety that Kirsten had never known.

"Lucky you."

"I tell myself that every day."

Kirsten took Kirby into her bedroom, which hadn't been touched at all. She put him on the bed and then went out, closing the door. "I don't want him escaping again," she said, coming back into the living room.

"I don't blame you," Cassie said.

Ross and Bear went to work on the door while Cassie helped Kirsten clean up her living room. As she put everything back in its place, she noted that not a single thing was missing. "That's weird," she said.

"What?"

"They didn't take anything. Why would they bother breaking in and then not taking a single thing?" She picked up a box off the floor and opened it. "I keep cash in this box for emergencies and it's still here. Every penny."

"That *is* strange."

"Who would do that?" She had a sneaking suspicion, but she wasn't about to say it out loud.

"Kids, probably," Cassie assured her.

"Door's fixed for now," Ross said. "Ye should get a new lock tomorrow.

"I'll call the hardware store in the morning. They'll send someone out to replace it."

"Good. Cassie, we should get going. I want to make one last check on the horses before bed."

"Okay. Call me if you need anything. Absolutely anything. I'll see you tomorrow," Cassie said, giving Kirsten a hug.

"We'll be out at the ranch bright and early," Kirsten said. "Gotta get that trail marked so it can be groomed."

She closed the door behind them and turned to find Bear standing close beside her. "I'll stay here in this room. If anyone tries to come in they'll soon wish they had no'."

She let his voice penetrate into her. She didn't know if it was the deep sound or the brogue, or something that was just uniquely him, but she felt safe. Protected, but in a way that wasn't suffocating. "I don't doubt it."

She took in his muscular frame and imagined what it would be like to be wrapped in it all night long. All at once she remembered he was watching her and she felt her skin go hot from the direction her thoughts had gone. "I'll get you some blankets and a pillow," she squeaked. "I hope you'll be comfortable on the couch." She moved past him quickly keeping her eyes on the floor.

"I've slept on the ground many a night, so I'll be fine."

She opened her bedroom door and Kirby bolted out. He stopped when he saw Bear, but after a brief once over, he sidled up to him, rubbing himself all over his leg. Bear bent down, picking him up and cradling the big cat under his chin.

"You like cats?" she said, surprised. She'd yet to meet a guy who liked Kirby.

"Aye. We had many back home."

"Had?"

"They did no' belong to anyone, so they could come and go as they pleased. Before we left, they'd gone off somewhere."

Kirsten could hear Kirby purring loudly. "He really likes you."

"They tell me I have a way with the animals," he chuckled.

"I'd say they're right." Bear was full of surprises. She wanted to know more about all of them. When they'd spoken before, he'd wanted to go back home, which disappointed her more than it should. If only he would stay. He was just the kind of guy she wanted. Tall, dark and handsome—exactly as she liked her men, but more than that he seemed genuine and kind. There didn't seem to be a false bone in his body. She was going to have to find out more about him from Cassie, or she could just ask him herself. She'd never been shy about asking questions, but it could wait. She didn't want to bombard him with questions tonight.

Kirsten retrieved the blankets and a pillow for him and then sat on the couch, hoping he'd join her.

"I like yer home, Kirsten. It suits ye."

"I guess it does. I've been living here ever since I moved back to Delight."

"Where did ye go?"

"I went to college in San Francisco," she said, getting up and moving towards the kitchen. "I'm going to make some tea. Would you like some?"

"I would," he replied.

"I had every intention of being a doctor until I realized that I wasn't very good at science. Then I thought I'd be a lawyer, but it wasn't my thing, so I got a liberal arts degree and came home." She put the kettle on, got out some mugs and the tea. "Since I didn't make it to graduate school, my parents gifted me with the tuition money and I used that to buy the shop along with Sue and Amy. They each have a quarter share in the store and I own half. So, it's my responsibility to make sure it succeeds."

"Where are yer mother and father now?"

"They live on the other side of the mountains in Reno." She leaned back on the kitchen counter waiting for the water to boil. She could feel herself relaxing. This had been a stressful night and she craved some calm.

"Do ye see them often?" Bear asked.

"I try to get over there at least once a month. It's not too far, but I've been so busy."

The water was finally boiling. She put the tea together and carefully carried the two mugs into her living room. She handed one to Bear.

"Thank ye. Now that ye've got me to help ye, perhaps ye can see them before too long."

"Perhaps."

He finally sat down beside her and she resisted the urge to move closer. The pull she felt towards him grew stronger every time she saw him and now here he was spending the night in her house. She had no doubt he'd be the perfect gentlemen, but she couldn't help wishing that maybe he wouldn't be.

Bear had his suspicions about Tim. Could he possibly have been the one to break in? It was good that Kirsten had agreed to let him stay. If Tim or anyone else tried to come through that door, they were going to have to get through Bear first. He didn't have a doubt in his mind that he could best any man in any fight.

It felt good to have someone to protect. It felt good to feel an attraction to a woman once again. These past few years were filled with turmoil leaving him little time for himself as he fought to keep what little was left of his home and family. He wanted to share that with her, but knew it would only lead to questions he wasn't able to answer. Maybe soon he'd know her well enough to tell her the truth about himself and his brothers. For now it was best left unsaid. They'd been lucky to stumble upon Cassie and Ross here in this new and unfamiliar time. He hadn't had much time to think about how strange it all was and perhaps that was a good thing. His brothers needed him to remain strong. He was the oldest and therefore the one responsible for their well-being here in the year 2019.

Kirby had climbed up on Bear's chest and was making himself at home by kneading away before finally settling down and closing his eyes. He hadn't stopped purring since Bear picked him up that first time. There was a certain honor that came along with the approval of a cat. A warm smile crossed his face as he stroked Kirby's silky, soft fur.

"Kirby's quite taken with you. He thinks you're special."

"I'm feeling quite special," he chuckled, being careful not to disturb Kirby.

That special feeling extended to the way Kirsten was looking at him. It wasn't the look of a friend or casual acquaintance. It was the look of a woman in need of a man. It was good that the cat was occupying the space where he would otherwise have placed Kirsten before kissing her soundly on those sweet lips that were teasing him with a smile.

"I'm going to grab some cookies from the kitchen or biscuits, isn't that what you call them in Scotland? Would you like some?" she asked.

"Aye. 'Tis just what I need." *To take my mind from the places it has wandered.*

"I'll be right back."

She wasn't far. He could see her from where he was, but he wanted her back—near him. The space around him felt empty without her. Even the weight of Kirby on his chest and his gentle purring did nothing to fill that emptiness. It was an emptiness he had been feeling for the past year. It had become so commonplace that he'd hardly noticed until now. Until he'd met Kirsten and that empty place began to fill with a warmth he'd thought he would never experience again.

"Here you go," she said as she handed him a steaming mug.

He placed it on the table next to him.

"I always have a cup of tea before bed," she confessed. "It helps me fall asleep."

"You do no' sleep well?"

"Not always. I have so much going on in my head that sometimes I can't turn it off. Does that ever happen to you?"

"It does. More often than no'."

"Well, hopefully the tea I made does the same for you tonight." She sipped her tea and glancing over the rim of her cup, asked, "Are you warm enough? I didn't even think about putting a fire in the wood stove and it is a little chilly in here, especially since the door was wide open for who knows how long."

"I can make it for ye," Bear offered.

"No. You stay right where you are. We don't want to disturb Kirby," she smiled.

Kirsten went to the wood stove and placed a few small logs inside before using an item he was unfamiliar with to light it. Once it was blazing away, she shut the door and moved back to the couch. "That should warm this place up quickly, but in the meantime, we can share this blanket. She draped a fuzzy, warm blanket over the two of them and Kirby, moving close enough that it wouldn't take much for him to reach out and touch her. He kept his arms and hands still. She moved closer still. This time he could feel the warmth of her body resting on his arm. An involuntary groan left his lips.

"Sorry," Kirsten said backing away.

"Nae. Come back. 'Tis fine."

"Are you sure? I don't want to make you uncomfortable."

Nothing about her being this close was comfortable, but he wouldn't change it for the world. He wanted her even closer still, but it wasn't his place to touch her or kiss her if it wasn't what she wanted. Did she want it? If he was reading the signs correctly, she did.

"I just thought our body heat would warm us up faster."

"I believe yer right." She only wished to be warm. She wanted nothing more.

She rested one slender hand on his arm and then her head on his shoulder. It was going to take every ounce of restraint he had not to lift her face to his for a kiss. A tight, confining sensation centered around these new pants he wore. They were useful for many things, but this wasn't one of them. He squirmed slightly trying to adjust his growing manhood, but to no avail. It was torture plain and simple. He would remain a gentleman no matter what his head was telling him to do. He sat perfectly still noticing that Kirsten's breathing had become slow and steady.

She had fallen asleep. He was either going to have to carry her to her bed or have the worst night of his life sitting here holding a cat and wrestling with thoughts of Kirsten, warm and sweet in his arms. He stayed that way as long as he could before moving Kirby with his free arm. The cat yawned, stretched and then sat staring at him from the arm of the sofa as he lifted Kirsten in his arms and carried her to her bed. He lay her down, covering her with a blanket. *Would it be so bad for me to lay here with her?* He shook himself out of the crazy fantasy flowing through his head and, taking one last look at her, left her room and closed the door behind him.

Once on the couch, he made himself comfortable before inviting Kirby to join him again. Kirby nestled in with his head in Bear's neck. It wasn't Kirsten, but he wasn't alone.

CHAPTER 9

The sound of birds chirping away in the pine trees outside her bedroom window roused Kirsten from her sleep. She checked her phone for the time and hopped out of bed. She quickly brushed her teeth and washed the sleep from her eyes before heading into the living room to the sweetest sight she'd seen in a very long time. There, curled up on her sofa, was a very rugged Highlander and one fuzzy orange cat, both sound asleep nose to nose. She snuck a photo of them with her cell phone. This was a memory she didn't want to forget.

"Ahem," she cleared her throat and Bear stirred. Kirby gave her an irritated look, as if to say, *How dare you disturb us?*

"Bear," she said, "It's time to wake up." She walked closer to the sofa, laying a hand on his arm.

Before she knew what was happening, he grabbed her wrist, pulling her down onto him.

"Bear, what are you doing?" she squealed, realizing this wasn't a playful wrestle.

"I'm sorry, lass. Ye startled me. I thought someone had come to break into yer home again." He sat up, but still held onto her.

Kirsten wasn't about to complain, she liked being so close. If she moved her head up the slightest little bit, their lips would touch. What would be wrong with that? She wanted to find out. She moved her head, just as he moved his and instead of kissing, he bonked his forehead on her nose.

"Ouch!" she squealed.

"I hurt ye. Forgive me." He jumped to his feet.

Kirsten imagined he wanted to get as far away from her as he could before anything else went wrong.

"It's okay, Bear. Really it is. It's my fault. I shouldn't have woken you. I mean, I should have woken you, but maybe not that way."

Bear scrubbed his hands through his hair. "I'm awake. Is yer nose alright?"

"It is," she smiled, enjoying the sight of him looking slightly rumpled from sleep. "We should get going. We've got a lot to do today. You can take a shower first if you like."

He headed towards the bathroom without saying a word.

"Towels are hanging up in there," she called to him and then the bathroom door closed behind him.

She picked up Kirby and brought him to the kitchen. "You ready to eat? I don't mind telling you I'm a little jealous that you spent the night in Bear's arms." With any luck at all that would be her in the not too distant future.

Kirsten and Bear stopped in at the ranch before heading out on foot to plot the course for what would become the cross-country ski race and the snowshoe race. They brought markers to place along the trail. Walter, Rose's husband, would be by later to make the path wider while grooming it at the same time.

It was a bright, sunny day. The air was crisp and cold and yesterday's snow had only turned out to be a light dusting. Despite the fact that someone had broken into her home yesterday, Kirsten wasn't feeling too worried about it. She'd slept really well last night. Something about knowing that Bear was right in the next room must have

101

penetrated her brain because her usual tossing and turning had disappeared for the night. She would have liked it even better if he'd joined her in the bed, but she didn't want to appear to be too forward. She was definitely attracted to him and if she wasn't mistaken he felt the same. In the shower this morning, she'd had a long conversation with herself. She wasn't going to throw herself at him. She was going to take it slow or at least at whatever pace felt right at any given moment. There was something very old fashioned about him and she wouldn't want to scare him off. For now she was happy to be trudging through the snow with him despite the frigid temperature.

They'd walked about a quarter of a mile placing small orange flags along the path before they started a slight incline. "This will be where the challenge starts. Most people will be beginners, so we don't want it to be too hard."

The hill gently sloped up to another flat length and then a steeper climb began again. She paused for a moment to take in the panoramic view, happy that this is what the tourists would see early in the race before they were too tired to appreciate it.

Bear turned to her. "Do ye need to rest before we go on?"

"Bear, I'm pretty fit. Remember I'm part of search and rescue and the ski patrol. I'm used to this. Maybe you need a rest," she teased, poking him in the side with her gloved finger.

"I could climb hills like this all day," he answered with a glint of mischief in his eyes and on his lips.

"Really? I'll race you to the top," she said, not giving him a chance to answer her. Her snowshoes dug into the snow as she attempted to race as quickly as possible to the top. Bear was right behind her and about to pass her when she stumbled and fell face first into the snow. Strong hands and arms lifted her from the snow and off her feet. Bear didn't place her back on the ground, instead tossing her over his shoulder and carrying her the rest of the way to the top before placing her on the ground once again.

"Wow! That was impressive," she gasped.

He shrugged his shoulders. "We did no' place any flags on the way up."

"Walt will figure it out." She placed a flag where she stood and glanced up at Bear. "Thanks for the ride," she said.

"My pleasure, lass."

"We've got about another half mile to go before we head back."

Bear brushed some snow from her cheeks. His fingers lingered there and Kirsten found herself leaning into them. Before she knew what was happening he dipped his head and placed a soft kiss on her lips. She was surprised, but pleased that he'd taken the first step. She kissed him back, wrapping her arms around his neck. They exchanged kisses for a few moments more before the sensible part of their brains kicked in and they separated.

"I've been wanting to do that for some time now," Bear said, his voice a deep rumble.

"Me, too," Kirsten concurred. "It was really nice."

"Shall we finish our task before we freeze in place?" he asked.

"Yes." She couldn't wait to finish. The thought of kissing Bear again was going to be on her mind from now until the moment when it happened again. This was going to be a great day.

He couldn't believe he'd been bold enough to kiss her. It was really all he'd been thinking about since he met her and now it had happened. He hoped it was something they'd continue when they finished mapping out the route for the race. They trudged uphill and down through the snow covered trees and finally after a particularly long downhill section the path curved around, ending not far from where they'd begun. They were both completely out of breath.

"It won't be so difficult once it's groomed," Kirsten said gasping for air.

They'd both fallen more than once, particularly on the downhill sections where the snow was deep and soft.

"Anyone who's a seasoned snowshoer will be just fine," Kirsten brushed the snow off of her jacket and then Bear's. She wrapped her arms around his waist. "Let's go back to the ranch. I'll make us some hot chocolate."

He pulled her in for the kiss he'd been thinking about for the past hour. Her cheeks were pink, her nose cold and her lips warm against his. He savored her kiss and then let her walk on ahead of him for a bit as his body reacted involuntarily to her nearness. The smile spreading across his face as he watched her felt good. He hadn't had much to smile about of late, but that seemed to be changing.

Once he had his body under control he was able to catch up to her with little effort.

"I love it when it's like this," she said. "The sky looks so blue with all the white snow on the ground and the fluffy white clouds in the sky."

"Ye like the cold then?"

"I don't mind it. What about you?"

"I prefer it warmer, but armed with these clothes, it was no' so cold."

They approached the ranch where Kade was leaving with Ross and Payton was mucking out stalls in the barn.

"Where are ye off to?" he called to his brother.

"The bakery," Kade answered. "I'm to work with Rose."

"Good luck to ye then. Do no' eat all the cookies," he warned with a teasing lilt to his voice. He was feeling good about everything and it showed.

Kade waved as the truck pulled out of the driveway.

"I'd like to learn to drive the truck," he said.

"You don't know how to drive?" Kirsten seemed surprised.

"Nae."

"How do you get around back home?"

"Walking or on horseback."

"Really? That sounds kind of nice, but I thought everyone who was old enough knew how to drive."

He wrapped an arm around her shoulder and led her to the front door of the ranch. It was a good thing she couldn't see his face.

✳

"Cassie!" Kirsten called when they entered.

"I'm in my office," Cassie answered.

"We were going to make hot chocolate, is that okay?"

"Sure. You know where everything is."

"I do." Kirsten led the way into the kitchen area and got out the cocoa, milk, and mugs they'd need. Bear watched everything she was doing with keen interest.

"You've had hot chocolate before, right?"

"I have no'."

"Well, you're in for a treat then." Where exactly did Bear live? He didn't know how to drive. He'd never had hot chocolate. It must be way out in the middle of nowhere. "If I got out a map of Scotland, could you show me where you're from. I'm curious."

"I do no' believe ye'll find it on a map."

"Even if it's not, you could pinpoint it based on some of the other places shown."

He shrugged his expansive shoulders, watching as she poured the hot chocolate into a mug in front of him. He went to reach for it, but she stopped him.

"It's not done yet." Kirsten found the bag of mini marshmallows Cassie kept in the cabinet next to the stove and dropped a few in each mug. "Now it's done. Go ahead. Taste it."

She watched intently as he took his first sip. A little bit of marshmallow stuck to his beard so she grabbed a napkin and wiped it off for him, holding his face in her hand as she did so. "You had a little marshmallow on you," she explained. "What do you think?"

"I think I like it," he said, licking more marshmallow from his lips.

Those lips. They'd been taunting her all day. She'd gotten her chance to sample a few kisses, but she wanted so much more than his lips. She wanted all of him. She sipped her drink, eyeing him over the rim of her cup. He was doing the same. If she wasn't in Cassie's house, she'd be on him in a matter of seconds, but that wasn't the case. He shared the cabin with his brothers so they couldn't go there. They were going to have to wait.

There was a knock at the door, interrupting her daydream.

"Can you get that?" Cassie called from her office.

"Sure."

Opening the door, Kirsten was surprised to see Tim standing there.

"Hey," he said.

"What's up?" she asked.

He looked past her to the counter where Bear was sitting. "I saw your car and I wanted to make sure you were okay after the break in last night."

"I'm fine. Bear stayed at the house with me." She knew it probably wasn't the best thing to tell him, but he didn't seem to want to let go even though he said he would.

His posture stiffened. "Do you really think that was a good idea? For all you know maybe it was him who broke into your house."

"That would be impossible. I was with him, here at the ranch until it was time for me to drive home."

"Oh." He hesitated. "Well, you shouldn't let him stay with you. You don't know anything about him. What will people in town think?"

"First, people in town have known me my whole life. Most of them are close friends so they won't *think* anything. He was there to protect me because I asked him to. And second, he's Ross's cousin and he's a good guy."

He didn't seem to have an answer for that. She saw a muscle ticking in his jaw, but he decided to drop it and change the subject. "Are you going to be coming to work later?" he asked.

"Shoot! I forgot today was my day on patrol." She glanced down at her watch. "I'll be in at my usual time."

"I'll see you then," he said. He turned back to her as she was closing the door. "Kirsten, be careful."

Be careful of what? she wondered. Working with Tim was going to be awkward. She'd have to see about changing her hours so that they didn't match up with his, but that might be difficult considering he was the snow safety team leader and technically her boss. She should have listened to her gut the first time he asked her out. Dating someone at work, especially the boss, was never a good idea.

"What did he want?" Bear asked, joining her near the door.

"He was worried about me after what happened last night." She peeked through the window to make sure he was gone. "You know, it's unusual that we have break-ins around here. We always say the sheriff has the easiest job in town because nothing ever happens in Delight."

"Hopefully that was the last of it." His tone was so reassuring. She decided to take a step forward into his arms. He pulled her close, she laid her head against his chest and listened to his steady heart beat. What was it about him that made her feel safe?

"You're right. One break-in isn't a crime spree. It doesn't hurt to be careful, but I'm not going to worry about it anymore."

They stood there a moment longer when reality started to interfere. "I have to go," she said, regret ringing in her ears.

"I'll go with ye," he whispered and she felt it down to her toes. This man was something else.

She smiled at the hopeful grin he was wearing.

"I'm afraid you can't. I've got to get ready for work and I can't take you with me."

"Will I see ye later?" he asked.

"I don't know. If I get through early enough I'll stop by."

"Who'll stay with you tonight?"

"No one. I'll be okay."

He didn't look convinced.

"I'll keep all the doors locked and if anything happens I'll call Ross and Cassie right away so you can come rescue me, okay?"

He nodded. Placing his large hand on the side of her face, he leaned in for the kiss she'd been waiting for. Nothing was rushing them now. They were inside of a warm house where they could relax and enjoy the feel of soft, warm lips tasting and exploring each other. She pressed herself up against him and was rewarded by the hard feel of a man aroused. Aroused by her. They lingered there for a moment before she reluctantly pulled away.

"Mmmm…" was about all she could say. He cocked his head to the side as she lightly brushed his lips with her fingertip. "I'll see you later."

Bear stood by the door reliving their kiss. He could still feel her lips as they glided across his. The feel of her silken tongue tangling with his caused him to groan out loud.

"Are you okay?" Cassie asked entering the room.

He stood facing the door for a moment longer. It was time to get his emotions and body under control.

"Bear?" she asked.

This time he turned to her. "I be fine, Cassie."

"Where's Kirsten?"

"She had to leave." He walked into the kitchen taking the two empty mugs with him. He examined the sink and having memorized what Cassie and Ross did to turn the water on, he did exactly that and rinsed out the two mugs.

"Here, you can put them in the dishwasher," Cassie said, showing him how. "You like her, don't you?"

He was sure it was obvious to anyone with eyes. "I do. Verra much."

Cassie clapped her hands and hopped up and down. "Yes! I knew you two would hit it off."

He was puzzled by her words, but he was getting used to all the new terms. He always listened carefully to everything being said in case there was a clue that would help him understand.

"You got the course all set for the races, right?"

"We did. Kirsten said Walt would take care of the final touches."

"Good. I'm feeling a whole mix of excitement and anxiety. I know everything is going to be great. I'm still a little apprehensive, but I'm going to try not to think about it."

"Tell me about Tim," Bear said as they stood at the kitchen counter.

Cassie refilled her coffee mug. "Well, I don't know a whole lot about him. He's only been here since November of last year. He works at the ski lodge coordinating the ski patrol and search and rescue. He doesn't really socialize much or I'd know a whole lot more."

"He's in love with Kirsten," he said. He could see it in his eyes when he spoke to her and hear it in his voice when he threatened Bear.

Cassie paused at that and considered it. "I don't know that I would call it love. He's been obsessed with her ever since they first met. He was always showing up unexpectedly at the oddest moments. It was like he was watching her all the time and knew exactly where she was going to be. Kirsten went out with him a few times, but there wasn't a connection for her and so she's been trying to let him down easy for a while now. He hasn't wanted to let go."

Bear thought about what she was telling him. It was good to know that Kirsten had never felt anything for the man, but it was disturbing that Tim didn't understand.

"She told him flat out the other night that she didn't want to date him anymore, but I guess he's not giving up that easily."

Bear was worried about Kirsten. It was possible Tim was capable of harming her and he couldn't allow that to happen. He'd stay as close as possible, but how could he when she was at work with Tim. "I'm worried about her working with him."

Cassie seemed to dismiss his concern with a shrug of her shoulders. "I wouldn't worry about that too much. There are other people there with them all the time. Besides, she can take care of herself and I think she's planning to change her schedule so they won't be there at the same time." Cassie glanced out the window, pulling the curtains back. "Ross is back."

"I hope Kade is a help to Rose. Everything is so new to him."

"Rose is great. She won't let him do anything he can't master."

The door opened and Ross joined them. "Kade's all set at the bakery. Rose said that Walt will be along to groom the trail in about an hour. Bear would you go with him? You know the trail since you helped Kirsten with it this morning."

"I'd be pleased to be of service," he said. He hadn't met Walt, but knew that he was married to Rose and he fixed the cars and trucks that everyone drove around Delight. He was also a handyman, as he'd been told by Cassie.

"He'll be by to pick you up."

Ross turned to Cassie. "What's for lunch?"

"Lunch? You just had breakfast."

"I should have asked Rose when I was there. She doesnae count the hours since I last ate." He winked at Bear to let him know he was only teasing his wife.

Cassie wrinkled her nose and brow, making a face that had both men laughing. "I'll heat up left overs from last night's dinner for the both of you. How does that sound?"

"It sounds like I would like that verra much," Ross said.

"As would I," Bear added.

Spending an afternoon with Tim was not high on the list of things Kirsten wanted to do, but this was her job and it was important. This winter alone they'd already rescued more than fifty skiers. Most were minor bumps and bruises, but there was always the occasional broken leg and sometimes life threatening injuries. She couldn't let her discomfort at being around Tim get in the way of doing what needed to be done. She closed her eyes and took a deep cleansing breath before entering the ski patrol offices.

"There you are," Tim said. "I was starting to wonder if you were going to show up today."

Kirsten looked at the clock. She was fifteen minutes early.

"I thought the two of us could work as a team today. We got a busload of newbie skiers here from a Bay Area high school. We'll need to keep an eye on them."

"I can do that alone. That'll free you up for any emergencies that might crop up." The last thing she wanted was to be tied to Tim all day.

It was clearer to her now more than ever that he wasn't the man for her. She felt suffocated by him. It was definitely not the way you should feel in a relationship. Now that she'd shared some delicious kisses with Bear she knew exactly what she wanted and it wasn't Tim. And yet, there he stood smiling at her like she was the only woman on earth.

"No. We're working together. I made the schedule. Someone else will handle the emergencies." The smile never left his face, but it did leave his voice.

"Okay. If you insist."

"I do."

This was going to be a long afternoon. The way Kirsten was feeling now didn't bode well for the rest of her time here. "We should get going then." At least they'd be surrounded by excited teens. That should keep them both busy.

As they walked towards the slopes, Tim seemed like he had something to say, but was having a hard time saying it.

"It's a good day for those kids to be up here," Kirsten said, trying to break the awkward silence.

"Clear skies, cold weather and freshly groomed slopes. What more could anyone ask for?"

"They're kids. I'm sure there must be something," she said.

"Kirsten, something's been bothering me."

Oh, no. Here it comes, she thought.

"That guy, Bear. And by the way, what kind of name is that? Who calls themselves Bear?"

"I'm sure it's short for his real name, which is Bearnard."

"Oh, still it's a weird name."

"Yes, so what did you have to say about Bear?"

"I don't like him. I don't like the way he looks at you. I think he's up to no good. I'm not sure what it is yet, but I'm going to find out and when I do, you'll see that I was right all along."

"Right about what?"

"That he's not the good guy you seem to think he is."

She stopped, looking at him and trying to read his face.

"Tim, it's not your job to worry about me. It never was. We are no longer dating and I can make my own choices." The idea that he was trying to protect her made her skin crawl.

"I know we're not dating, but I'm still concerned about you. I can't just turn that on and off. You're blinded by this guy."

"Tim! Stop. I can take care of myself and I'd appreciate it if you'd stay out of my business. Understood?"

He didn't answer her. He just turned and headed up the mountain. As a matter of fact, he had nothing at all to say to her for the rest of the day. Even when she spoke to him about work related matters, he ignored her. If he was trying to punish her, it wasn't working. Kirsten was more than happy to receive the silent treatment from him.

CHAPTER 10

*D*elight was looking good. The town was decked out in fairy lights, giant snowflakes and beautiful art that decorated every empty space. The town square had been set up for a snowman building contest. The shop owners had donated all sorts of items that people could use to dress their snowmen and women.

Rose scurried from one end of the bakery to the other. Kade was busy in the kitchen cutting out the cookies for the festival. Walt was busy grooming more trails. The ski shop was attaching race bibs to applications. Everything was running smoothly.

"I can't believe we haven't run into any problems," Kirsten said.

"Shhh... Don't say that. You'll jinx it."

"Don't be silly, Amy. I have no worries at all. Everyone has done an amazing job getting the festival up and running."

"I can't help it. I'm a worrier and I'm superstitious."

"You'll see. It's all going to go off without a hitch." Kirsten's heart skipped a beat as Bear came through the door.

"Good day to ye, lassies." His cheerful voice and relaxed demeanor was just what they needed.

"Hi, Bear," Amy said, elbowing Kirsten.

Was she that obvious?

"What can I do to help ye?" he asked coming to stand beside Kirsten.

It was like he had a vibrating force field around his body that was affecting Kirsten's ability to speak or think.

Amy's glance was darting back and forth between the two of them. "We're attaching these bibs to the race applications, but we got a shipment in of water and snacks, could you possibly make sure it's all there. We wouldn't want to be short anything."

Bear placed his hand on Kirsten's back. The sensation went straight through her body, penetrating her inner core and leaving her weak in the knees. "Thank you," she managed to blurt out. She wasn't thanking him for counting water, but for giving her a feeling she hadn't experienced in ages.

"Would ye mind showing me?" he asked.

"What?" Her brain was in a fog and it was all courtesy of Bear.

"The water. Can ye show me what ye wish me to do?"

"Oh, sure. Amy, I'll be right back."

"Take your time." Amy gave her a knowing smile.

Kirsten scowled back at her. What did Amy think she was going to do back there? What did *she* think she was going to do?

They were no sooner through the stock room door than Bear took her in his arms and she was more than happy about it.

"I've missed ye," he said.

"Mmm..." Places all over her body were tingling. Places that shouldn't be tingling here at work.

"Mmm... ye say. Does that mean ye missed me as well?"

"I think it does." It had only been a few short hours since they'd been together, but that was long enough.

"What's to be done about it?"

"Kiss me and find out."

She didn't have to tell him twice. He rained hot, sweet kisses on her mouth, her neck, the place where her shirt opened in a vee exposing her cleavage and then back to her mouth. She'd never ever been kissed like this before. She completely forgot where she was or what they were supposed to be doing as she pressed her body against hard muscle and a completely aroused man. His hands were every-where. So many sensations coursed through her body and all of them were good. No, they were amazing. Bear knew exactly what to do and where to do it. She was in ecstasy. He lifted her atop the boxes and she wrapped her legs around his waist.

"I want ye, lass."

Those four little words almost sent her over the edge. She was so turned on by Bear she was pretty sure she'd let him make love to her right here and now on top of these boxes.

The bell over the front door rang and she could hear Amy talking to someone. She pulled Bear's lips to hers and kissed him with all the passion she had inside of her for one last kiss. "We've got to stop. There's a customer out there."

The voices were getting closer. They were coming in the back room. She shoved Bear away from her and hopped off the box, straightening her clothes. Bear turned away, facing the boxes as though he was counting them.

"There you are," Cassie said, coming through the door. "Amy was trying to tell me you left."

Behind her Amy was grinning like a fool. "Oh, ummm... no, I just came back here to check on Bear. He is, ummm... helping." That sounded ridiculous but she honestly couldn't remember why they were in here.

"Bear, you're working hard," she said.

He looked back over his shoulder, masking any emotion he may have been feeling.

Kirsten fought to control her breathing. She was out of breath from her extra curricular activities with Bear. Damn why did Cassie have to show up now?

"You look a little peaked," Cassie said. "Are you feeling okay? Do you have a fever?"

"I'm fine. I was just moving some boxes around."

"That's what Bear's for."

She wanted to say Bear was for so much more, but that would be weird.

"Was there something you needed?" Kirsten asked doing her best not to sound like Cassie was bothering her.

"I was just checking in to make sure everything is in place. I've got my list and I'm going through town checking things off. You know how I love to do that." She waved her clipboard around. There must be ten pages of notes on that thing. She wasn't sure how Cassie kept it all straight.

"I do. What's on the list for me?"

She flipped through some pages. "Race applications, bibs, water, snacks."

"Check, check, check and check."

"You're the best," Cassie said as she made her notes. "Is the race site all set?"

"As far as I know it should be good unless it snows. If it does, we'll need to do more grooming."

"Great." She made a few more notes then looked up with a big grin on her face.

"Well, I'm off to the inn."

"See you later then."

"Oh, I'm inviting everyone who's been working so hard on this over for dinner tonight. Will you be able to come?"

"I'll be there," she said casting a sly glance back to Bear.

"Okay. Later alligator."

"Later."

Kirsten drew in a deep breath as Cassie walked out. She listened to her saying goodbye to Amy and then heard the front door close.

"Phew! That was close."

Bear laughed and she joined him.

"Sorry about that," Amy said peeking in the doorway.

"Why? What do you think we're doing back here?"

"Counting water and snacks," Amy said, giggling as she turned away.

"I guess we should get to work." Kirsten couldn't hide the disappointment in her voice.

"Later," Bear said. "Isn't that what ye say?"

Kirsten laughed. "Yes, it is. Later."

irsten closed the shop early so Sue and Amy could join them for dinner. It was a small town and they usually rolled up the sidewalks at around six in the evening, but tonight they closed even earlier. She had Bear in her car as they drove to the ranch and it was all she could do not to pull over and ravish the man. He was smoking hot and her mind was going places it shouldn't. She'd better focus on her driving no matter how distracting her passenger was.

The ranch was lit up inside and out. Ross had strung faerie lights all over the buildings, barns, fencing and trees giving it a magical appearance.

Rose and Walter were already here, as evidenced by their truck in the driveway. Kirsten had no sooner parked than Avery Winter pulled in, followed by Amy and Sue. Joe Evans, their official photographer was already here taking photos for the town website. Mike and Amanda, Cassie's former neighbors, drove down the hill to join them and it seemed they brought a case of wine from their winery.

"This is really nice," Kirsten said to the group. They all greeted each other with smiles and hugs.

Bear stayed close by Kirsten's side, which was fine with her. She smiled up at him and he winked in return. They had a little secret. A covert little something that it seemed only Amy knew about.

Inside the house, it was warm and bright, filled with laughter and chattering, happy voices. Ross handed them each a glass of wine and Kirsten clinked glasses with Bear before turning to face towards the others. He stayed behind her, playfully cupping her backside. She swatted his hand away, but then held and squeezed it, making sure he knew she'd liked it.

Cassie cleared her throat and clinked the side of her glass. "Can I get everyone's attention for a minute. I just wanted to say a few words." The room quieted and Cassie continued. "When we started talking about this last year, we weren't sure we could pull this off, but I'm happy to say that by everyone pitching in and doing their part, this is going to be an amazing event. Avery's inn is full, we're all booked up here at the ranch. We sold more tickets than I dreamed possible for the evening parties. We've got so many participants in the races and other activities. I'm beyond proud of all of us. We did it! We saved Delight!"

Everyone clapped and cheered.

"We couldn't have done any of it without you and Ross," Rose said. The others all agreed. She raised her wine glass. "I'd like to make a toast. To Ross and Cassie."

Everyone drank and Cassie wiped a happy tear from her eyes. Ross wrapped an arm around her shoulders pulling her close and kissing the top of her head.

Kirsten felt Bear tense behind her. "Is everything okay?" she asked.

"Aye." He was gazing out the front window of the house.

She followed his gaze and noted a car parked across the road with its headlights on. The car remained in place and soon the headlights went off.

"I wonder who that is?" she asked, glancing up at Bear. His face was without expression. He continued watching and waiting, but for what? She took one more look around the room and it seemed they weren't missing any of the group working on the festival. Everyone was accounted for. If whoever it was out there was coming in, she'd know soon enough.

It didn't appear Bear was willing to wait. "Kade, Payton, come with me."

The brothers were through the door in a flash. No one else at the party seem to notice. They were all much too busy chatting with each other about the festival and how their businesses were benefitting from Cassie's great idea.

Kirsten moved closer to the window and watched closely as Bear and his brothers padded through the snow in a low crouch. The lights outside weren't hiding their presence from Kirsten, but she wasn't sure if the occupant of the vehicle parked across the road had the same view. They skirted around the back of the car and came up on either side. Bear pulled the car door open and grabbed the occupant, pulling the man out and pushing him up against the car. Kade and Payton came around to stand on either side of him. Kirsten was squinting so hard to try and see who it was that she was giving herself a headache. She didn't know what was being said, but before too long, Bear shoved the unknown person back into their car, which started up and sped away in record time.

When they returned, Kirsten pulled Bear into Cassie's office and closed the door. "Are you crazy? They could have had a gun or some other weapon." Her heart was racing in her chest at the thought of Bear being injured or killed.

"Tim hunts ye," he said, placing a calming hand on her shoulder.

"Tim? Was that who it was?"

"Aye. I told him to stay away from ye or he'd answer to me and my brothers. He seemed frightened enough to do as I suggested."

"Oh." She wasn't sure what to think. Sure, she wanted Tim to stay as far away from her as possible, but she didn't think Bear needed to threaten him. "I don't think you should have done that. I'm perfectly capable of taking care of myself. I don't need you interceding on my behalf."

"He follows ye."

"You don't know that. Maybe he was just joining us here for dinner. Maybe Cassie invited him."

"I do no' believe that to be the case. She did no' wait for him before thanking everyone."

Bear had a point, but she wasn't sure how she felt about it. "I still have to work with him, you know."

"I do no' believe ye should." he said.

"Just who do you think you are telling me what I can and cannot do? I love my job. I keep people safe and I'm not letting some jerk stand in my way." He flinched and she realized that Bear thought she meant him. "I'm sorry. That came out wrong. Tim's the jerk. Not you."

"He's a danger to ye," he said.

"In what way aside from being incredibly annoying?"

"I do no' know. If ye insist on working with him, I will stay close."

"Look, you don't have to worry about me. I already told you that." She was feeling irritated by his insistence on protecting her. It wasn't that she didn't enjoy all the strong, manly parts of him, but this was taking things too far. "Please, don't interfere in my life."

A brief look of hurt crossed his face before he wiped away any show of emotion. She couldn't read him. Had she angered him? She hoped not, but she had to get through to him. If any harm came to Tim, he'd be held responsible and she didn't want to be the cause.

"I don't want to talk about this anymore. We should get back to the party."

Why was she being so stubborn? Bear thought he'd done the right thing. No. He knew he'd done the right thing. This Tim was a threat to Kirsten and for some reason she was choosing not to believe it. The fact that he was now out of favor with her was something he could deal with. He could not, however, deal with any threat to her well-being. He would protect her. It was something he was good at and he could do it without her knowledge.

"Yer lady is no' happy with ye," Kade said as Bear joined him and Payton.

"She does no' ken what's good for her," he replied.

"The lassies are different here, Bear. Ye can no' tell her what to do."

He watched from across the room as Kirsten approached Cassie. He imagined she was asking about Tim. Cassie shook her head to whatever question Kirsten asked and then the two of them walked into the kitchen.

"We must protect her, Kade."

"I trust yer judgment. I'll help in any way I can."

"As will I," Payton added.

Those around them were talking and laughing. They were a happy lot. His thoughts returned to his own time when his friends and neighbors gathered for a *ceilidh*. Music, dancing, food and good cheer were common at one time in his life. Seeing these happy revelers made him more sure than ever that he had to return home and bring good fortune back to his people. He was the chieftain of his estate before it became English property and as such he had a responsibility to those who relied on him.

Kade seemed to be reading his mind. "Ye ken ye were no' to blame for what happened."

"I was. I am."

"I do no' believe it and neither does Payton."

"Kade is right," Payton said.

"Payton, ye lost yer wife and bairn. 'Twould no' have happened if our home was as it once was. I blame myself."

"Yer a fool to do so," Payton said. "If anyone was to save them, it should have been me." His voice was harsh and the emotions were just there, under the surface, but he kept his composure. "Yer too hard on yerself. There are many things in our lives that we have nae control over. What happened to our family, to our home, was no' our fault. We were the victims. The English are to blame."

"I do no' wish to be a victim," Bear said.

"Ye three look quite serious," Ross said, joining them.

"We were discussing our home." Kade explained

Ross looked to each man, understanding clear on his face. "'Tis a great loss. One that cuts deep. I ken how ye feel. I was like ye nae so long ago, but coming to Delight and meeting Cassie showed me that I could move on. There's nothing ye can do to change Scotland's fate, Bear. Here with us, ye can build a new life. A good one. Lamenting the past willnae do ye good."

Perhaps Ross was right, but Bear didn't feel he was able to let go just yet. It might take him some time and if there ever was a chance he could go back, he would do it in a heartbeat.

"So, if you didn't invite Tim, why was he parked out there?" Kirsten asked Cassie as they were taking food out of the oven and preparing platters for the table.

"I don't know, but I'm glad Bear and his brothers had a little chat with him. His behavior scares me, I'm not going to lie."

Should she be scared, too? No. That was silly. Tim was annoying, not dangerous. "Threatening Tim was the wrong thing to do. Who does stuff like that?"

"He's worried about you."

"It's not his job to worry about me."

"He can't help it. He cares about you and where he comes from that's they way things are done."

She thought about that. On the one hand she did like the way he made her feel, that protective aura he had. "It's not that I don't appreciate the thought, but I really can take care of myself. I've told him that and he either just doesn't get it or he has chosen not to listen to me."

"Look, in his time…" Cassie began and ended abruptly.

"What?" Kirsten was confused. What did she mean *in his time?*

"That's not what I meant to say," Cassie stammered.

"Where's your head at? That was a really weird thing to say." Kirsten read Cassie's body language. She swiped at her nose, rubbed her forehead and then twirled her hair around and around her finger. She'd known her long enough to gather that she had meant what she said. She'd just slipped up.

Cassie took a long, slow breath in. "I'm sorry. I've just had so much stuff on my mind with the festival."

"It's okay. I mean I wouldn't have said anything, but in a sense, it fits. He does seem out of place. Everything seems so new to him. I know he's from Scotland, but for goodness sake, they aren't in the dark ages over there."

"Kirsten, if I told you something related to what we're talking about, would you think I'd lost my mind?" Cassie was looking sheepish again and that concerned her.

"I won't know until you tell me." Her stomach was doing back flips. Maybe she didn't want to know.

"Okay. Here goes nothing. Bear and his brothers are from the year 1747. They time traveled here in an avalanche." She blurted the words out so fast that Kirsten thought she may have misunderstood her.

"What? Wait, you aren't serious are you?" Her hands were shaking and her heart felt like it was about to beat right out of her chest.

"I am." Cassie looked up at the ceiling and then towards the door as though she was trying to find a place to crawl away and hide.

Kirsten examined her friend and could see no indication that she was lying to her. "I don't believe you."

"I didn't think you would, but I thought you should know. Please don't share that information with anyone else." Cassie chewed on her lip awaiting Kirsten's reply.

"I won't. I wouldn't want them to think you're losing it." Maybe she'd had a little too much wine. She'd never known Cassie to drink so much that she didn't make any sense, but there was a first time for everything.

"You can believe me or not, but I'm telling you to pay attention, I think you'll figure it out."

Kirsten thought back to the avalanche where the three men appeared out of nowhere. She'd been focused on the slope, making sure it was clear and she hadn't seen them. Then once the avalanche was in motion, there they were. She peeked into the living room to see Bear and his brothers huddled together in conversation with Ross.

"Does Ross know about this?" she asked.

"He does."

"And he believes it?"

"Yes."

"If you're playing a joke on me, Cassie, it's not a very good one," she warned.

"It's no joke." Cassie was sounding quite serious and she was looking right at Kirsten now. Her eyes never wavered.

"You can't possibly expect me to believe you. Time travel isn't real."

"All I'm saying is you should be observant. You might be surprised by what you find out."

Kirsten shook her head and waggled her finger at Cassie. "I need a drink."

She walked back into the living room and helped herself to a glass of whisky. What on earth had gotten into Cassie?

CHAPTER 11

"This was so much fun," Kirsten said, hugging Cassie first and then Ross. "We should do this more often. We don't have to wait for a big event to get everyone together."

"You're right. Let's get through the festival first and then we'll plan something." Cassie was leaning heavily on Ross and Kirsten could see she was dead tired and needed some rest.

"Good night," she said as Cassie closed the door behind her.

Bear stood on the porch looking out at the lights and Kirsten wondered at a grown man looking so enchanted by faerie lights. Cassie had put thoughts in her head that would have never been there otherwise and now she was seeing things. The lights were beautiful, of course he'd appreciate them. "Pretty, aren't they."

"Like hundreds of twinkling fireflies," he replied, his voice filled with awe.

"I'm heading home. I'll see you tomorrow." Their argument earlier was hanging between them, but she didn't know of any way to make it better right now.

"I'm coming with ye," he announced, looking away from the lights for the first time as he spoke.

"I don't remember inviting you." She was feeling annoyed with him. With men in general. What was it with them always thinking she needed them to watch out for her?

"'Tis best if I do." His voice was quiet and she wondered what his ulterior motive might be.

"For who?" she snapped.

"For ye." Again the quiet, calm she had come to appreciate in him.

"Really. Why is that?" She had no more fight left in her. She was tired and she wanted to go home. Alone.

"I will be there if Tim..."

"No more about Tim, please. He's not going to do anything to harm me. I've never worried about that with him. I admit he's having a hard time dealing with the fact that I'm not interested in him, but that doesn't mean he'd try to hurt me."

Bear opened his mouth to speak again, but she cut him off.

"Good night, Bear." She marched off towards her car unaware that Bear was right behind her.

"I'll sleep in the car. I will no' bother ye."

His voice in her ear startled her. "You're stealthy like a cat," she said, spinning to face him.

"Do no' be angry with me, please."

His sad smile softened her heart. "I'll be fine. I promise." She placed a soft hand alongside his cheek and he held it there. She could really fall hard for this guy. She needed to pace herself.

He walked her to her car and watched as she backed out of the driveway. Her headlights illuminating him made Bear look surreal. She thought again about what Cassie had told her. It couldn't possibly be. She stopped, rolling down her window.

"Hey, Bear," she called to him. His long strides had him at her window in a flash. "How'd you get here?"

His puzzled expression was followed by a moment or two of thought. "The same way anyone else would get here."

"You didn't just appear out of nowhere, did you? Did you take a plane, a boat, train, bus? How'd you get here?" It wasn't a tough question, but he seemed to be unable to answer her. After a moment or two of watching his eyes moving up and down and side to side she'd had enough and rather than wait for him to make something up she began rolling her window up. "Never mind," she muttered as it closed completely. She had a lot to think about and some research to do on time travel, as nutty as that seemed.

He moved back away from the car as she continued backing up and stood watching her as she began to drive away. Kirsten hoped he would go back to his cabin and get a good night's sleep. She on the other hand didn't know how she was going to get any sleep in at all. Her mind was reeling at the prospect of a time traveling Highlander.

Bear trudged through the snow that led to the small porch and front door of the cabin. Kirsten's final question to him had been unexpected. So unexpected in fact that he wasn't able to answer her. Did she know something about where they were from? It seemed she might. He'd been told not to say anything to anyone because they would never believe him and so he'd been careful not to do anything that might cause suspicion.

He'd been very aware of his reactions to all the new things he was experiencing, but gazing at the faerie lights all around the property might have been his downfall. They were magical little lights and he had no idea how or why they worked, but they had mesmerized him. It must have been what caused Kirsten's suspicious questioning.

"I thought ye'd be with Kirsten," Kade said, seeming surprised when Bear entered the cabin.

"She did no' wish me to go with her," Bear said. "She does no' believe Tim will harm her." He sank heavily into the sofa feeling as though he'd done nothing wrong, but knowing that somehow he had.

"She may be right," Kade said.

He had no wish to discuss this with Kade. He was young and inexperienced. He wouldn't know what Bear understood to be true. Tim was a threat. He changed the subject. "Where's Payton?"

"He's sleeping. This has been hard on him."

"I ken it. He's lost everything and now here we are in this place." Bear felt guilty. He'd been so busy thinking about Kirsten that he'd ignored Payton.

"'Tis hard to believe." Kade shook his head.

"We'll get back home somehow." Bear felt defeated, but he would be strong for his brothers. They needed him to lead them.

"I'm happy here," Kade said.

"We don't belong here. We must go back." He knew he sounded a bit defensive, but staying was never the plan and Kade was too young to make that decision.

"Why? There's no one there who'll truly miss us," Kade pointed out.

Kade was right, but Bear was loathe to agree with him. "'Tis true, but I'm the chieftain, 'tis my duty to take care of those who remain."

"Ye've cared for everyone for as long as I can remember. Let them care for themselves. The outcome will no' be so different," Kade scoffed, something younger brothers were good at.

"What do ye mean? Do ye no' believe I can save the people we left behind?" It was a question he asked more of himself than Kade. There was anger in the question, despair and a sense of hopelessness. It tore at Bear, leaving a knot in the pit of his belly. And then Kade said the words he knew to be true.

"Ye can no'. 'Tis a lost cause."

He wouldn't give up. He couldn't. Even if it meant going back and losing his life to the dragoons. He had to try. His honor depended on it.

"Whisky?" Kade asked. "'Twill help ye sleep."

Bear took the glass Kade offered him. He doubted that it would help at all. The thoughts flying to and fro in his head wouldn't allow him to sleep. In the past his worries centered around his home and his people. Now they involved another—a woman who had wormed her way into his heart in no time at all. His ma had always told him that when he found the woman meant for him he'd know without question who she was. He'd known from the instant he'd set eyes on Kirsten. Why did he have to come all this way through time to find her? It was one of the many unanswered questions that would haunt his sleepless night.

"I believe I'll sit up here and sip my whisky for a while. Sleep does no' wish to claim me yet."

"If ye do no' mind, I'll sit with ye," Kade said.

Bear loved his brothers, but he had a soft spot in his heart for Kade. He was the youngest and as such had followed Bear around like a wee pup as he grew. He had grown into a fine man and one who seemed keenly aware of the fact that his brother needed him right now. He was wise beyond his years and despite his near death experience running from the dragoons, Kade had recovered well and Bear had no doubt that left here in this time, he would thrive.

He wasn't so sure about Payton. He was harder to read. His grief had turned him into a silent shell of the man he'd once been. He rarely seemed to care enough about anything to speak, which concerned Bear. He had no experience with losing a wife or child. Losing both was more than any one man should ever have to bear. It wasn't that he hadn't ever lost a loved one. They'd lost their ma and da, but while that was hard, it was said there was no loss greater than the loss of a child. He could see that written on Payton's face every time he looked at him. He prayed his brother's grief would lessen with time. Bear would be by his side until it did.

"It's only me, Kirby." Kirsten closed and locked the door behind her. She'd left some lights on, so she was able to clearly see Kirby sprawled out on the sofa. He raised his head acknowledging her presence before returning to his prone position and whatever it was that cats dreamt about.

Her nerves were a little on edge as she made her way through each room, glancing in corners and closets before heading to her bedroom where she did the same. "You're being silly," she said, reprimanding herself for allowing Bear to frighten her with his warnings about Tim.

She changed into her pjs and headed back to the living room to sit with Kirby. She was about to turn on the television when her phone buzzed. "Ugh!" She really wasn't in the mood for a phone conversation, but she thought it best to at least see who it was.

Tim's name was front and center on her screen. She sent it through to voicemail. A few seconds later, she got a text from him wanting to make sure she was alright. She didn't answer and a few seconds later another text came through and then another and another.

She picked up the phone and dialed Tim's number.

"Tim, what is wrong with you? I'm fine," she said.

"I'm worried about you. Those three thuggy Scots were trying to scare me away from Cassie's house earlier. I don't trust them, especially Bear. I've been watching them. They're up to something." She heard the paranoia in his voice and it was unsettling. "I don't know what it is, but they think if they can scare me away they'll be able to get away with whatever it is they're planning."

"Why were you sitting out there anyway. Why didn't you just come in the house? You would have been welcome there."

"I was watching those guys to see what they were up to."

"They were eating dinner along with everyone else." As much as she tried to control it, her irritation with him was showing. "Stop being ridiculous. They're not planning anything. I told you they're Ross's cousins. They're here helping out with the festival. You don't have anything to worry about."

"Something tells me I do. There's something off about Bear. I don't know what it is, but I plan on finding out."

Kirsten felt herself getting impatient with Tim, but she controlled it. "Look, I'm really tired. I'm going to get some sleep and you should, too. We're all going to be extremely busy during the festival."

"Are you sure you're okay. I could come by and hang out with you for a while." The desperation in his voice worried her, but not enough to invite him over.

"I'm fine. I don't need you or anyone to come hang out. I've got Kirby and the two of us are safe and secure."

"Kirsten, just so you know, I'm going to keep an eye on you. I'm really worried about that guy."

She gritted her teeth. It was bad enough when Bear thought she needed to be watched over, but now Tim was joining in on the fun. "You will not keep an eye on me. You will stop calling me at all hours. You will stop following me and we'll go back to being colleagues. Nothing more. Is that clear?"

"Fine," And then he hung up.

She'd always thought having two guys interested in her at the same time might be kind of fun, but in actual fact it was anything but. She decided to follow her own advice and hit the hay, but before she got a chance to move from the sofa, her phone rang again. This time it was Amy.

"Hey, you know I'm living vicariously through you," Amy said. "Spill the beans lady. Why didn't you let Bear go home with you?"

"Amy, I do believe you're trying to get me laid."

"That's kind of crass, don't you think?" Amy said, a teasing lilt to her voice. "But yes, I am."

"We had a small disagreement about something. I need to slow it down with him anyway."

"Why? I say just go for it."

"Amy, let's focus on you. Which of our local bachelors do you want? I hear there's a winter formal at the high school next month…"

Amy screamed with laughter. "You're hilarious! You're never going to let me live that down are you? It was only that one time and he was twenty-one!"

"I'm just saying, instead of coaching me, why don't you find your-self a man."

"You know how hard that is to do around here."

"There could be some eligible bachelors coming up for the festival this weekend."

"Gawd, I hope so!"

"I'll be on the look out for you."

"Thanks. So what happened with Bear?"

"He threatened Tim. Told him to stay away or he'd be sorry."

"Oh! That's hot. He's staking his claim to his woman," Amy laughed.

"I'm no one's personal property, Amy." Why was she getting so worked up over this?

"You're no fun. I'm kidding," Amy assured her.

"Sorry. I'm feeling a little sensitive at the moment." She fiddled with a loose thread on her shirt. She just wanted this to stop. She wanted Tim to leave her alone and she wanted Bear to... well, she wanted Bear for a whole different reason.

"Didn't Tim threaten him first? In the store?"

"He did." She realized that Bear had every right to be suspicious of Tim's motives. Had there been other confrontations? Did Bear know about Tim's wild accusations?

"And you never told Tim to knock it off, did you?" Amy asked, making total sense.

"No, but he's only one guy. Bear had his brothers to back him up."

"I don't know. I'd be flattered by all this attention."

"You can have it. I don't want any Neanderthal men getting into a fight over me. It's not as fun as you seem to think." The amount of grumpiness in her voice surprised her.

"I'm sorry. I didn't know it was bothering you that much. I mean, I knew it was bothering you, but not enough to get you into such a bad mood."

"I'm not in a bad mood. I guess I'm feeling a little vulnerable right now. I did something I've never done when I got home tonight. I checked all the closets and under the bed for intruders."

"Or ghosts and things that go bump in the night."

"Thanks, Amy. I'll never get to sleep now."

"I'm on my way over. We'll have a slumber party. Oh, and warn Kirby, I'm bringing Otto with me."

Amy hung up the phone and Kirsten couldn't lie. She was relieved she'd have someone in the house with her tonight. It would settle her nerves. Amy was always a lot of fun and if anyone could get her out of this weird mood she was in, it would be her friend.

About thirty minutes later, she heard Amy's car pull into the driveway and she went to the door, opening it to find Tim getting out of his car.

"I told you not to worry about me," she said, unable to hide the annoyance in her voice.

"Sorry, I had to see for myself that you were okay. After the break in the other night I've been worried it might happen again."

"It's not going to. It was a random event. The sheriff said it was probably some kids passing through town. They were probably looking for drugs or something and since I don't have any, they left empty handed. Now, you can turn yourself around, get back in your car and go home. Amy's staying here with me tonight." As if on cue, Amy's car pulled in next to Tim's. Kirsten said a silent thank you to the heaven's above. For the first time, she let herself worry about what might have happened if Amy hadn't come over.

"Hi, Tim," she said, getting out of her car. "What are you doing here?" She glanced up on the porch at Kirsten.

"He was just leaving," Kirsten said.

Amy grabbed her bag from the trunk of her car and headed for the door. Not willing to leave his departure to chance, Kirsten peeked through the curtains of her living room and was shocked to see Tim standing there staring at the house long after she'd closed and locked the door.

"Should I go tell him to scram?" Amy asked.

"I don't know. He's been so weird since I told him I didn't want to date him anymore."

"I'll go out and send him on his way. I left Otto in the car. Thought I should give Kirby a minute to get used to me being here, but I can see he's already fled to your bedroom."

"No. Wait. I think he's leaving." Sure enough, he got in his car and was gone before Amy could get to the door.

"I'll be right back with Otto."

Kirsten watched her friend retrieve her little dog, glancing this way and that as she did.

"It's a little warmer than usual tonight. It's still pretty dang cold, but I can still feel my nose, which tells me we're at just about the right temp for snow."

Kirsten smiled an indulgent smile at Amy. She loved that girl. Aside from Cassie, she'd known Amy the longest. Between them and Sue, she had some really amazing friends. She felt incredibly lucky to have all of them in her life. "Hopefully only a light dusting, please."

"As if you can order that kind of thing." Amy took her jacket off and then her boots. As was their routine, she came already dressed in her pajamas. She grabbed some blankets and pillows, placing them on the sofa and then pulled some sodas and popcorn from her backpack.

"Amy, what do you think of Bear?" Kirsten asked. Despite her off the wall sense of humor, Kirsten valued Amy's opinion.

"Do you really need to ask? He's a hottie and I'm jealous that he likes you better than me."

"That's not what I mean. Do you think he seems a little out of place here." Kirsten was still bugged by what Cassie shared with her. She'd promised not to say anything, and she wouldn't.

"In Delight? Maybe a little, but I don't think he's from a ski village back home." Amy dug into the popcorn and then handed it to Kirsten.

"He's comfortable in the snow though," Kirsten observed.

"I'd say so. Why do you ask?" Amy searched the pillows until she found the remote control hidden under one of them.

"I'm just wondering if you've noticed anything weird about him."

"Not a thing, but my perception could be clouded by his gorgeousness."

Kirsten couldn't help but laugh. Amy was the funny one of their group. She could always be counted on to lighten the mood when necessary. Now was one of those times. She thought about her argument with Bear. She had probably overreacted. He hadn't really done anything wrong. She owed him an apology. For now, Kirsten decided to set her worries aside and enjoy time with Amy. "You want to watch a movie?"

"Sure. Something fun and romantic."

"Okay." They sat together on the sofa, Otto snuggled between them, and channel surfed until they found what they were looking for. Oddly enough it was about a woman who meets a man and discovers he is from another time. Kirsten decided to take mental notes and compare them to what she was seeing with Bear.

CHAPTER 12

The day of the winter festival had finally arrived and the town was packed. Guests were checking in at the inn, the ranch and the ski shop. Kirsten stopped in at the bakery to grab a quick cup of coffee and a snack and was thrilled to see a line out the door to buy Rose's special WinterFest cookies. Kade was happily helping out behind the counter, smiling and chatting with the customers. Rose had given him a crash course on helping the customers while she manned the cash register. Even Walt had taken some time to help out.

"How's it going? As if I need to ask." Kirsten said.

"Amazing! I can't believe it. I may be up all night baking more cookies," Rose said, handing some change to a woman who had purchased a dozen cookies.

"I'll help ye, if ye need me," Kade offered.

"You're a dear. We'll see how many cookies we have left later today." Rose turned back to Kirsten. "Coffee?"

"I can get it." Kirsten stepped behind the counter, grabbed a to go cup and filled it.

"Get yourself something to eat," Rose ordered. "You're going to need to be well nourished."

Kirsten grabbed her favorite chocolate croissant. "Thanks, Rose." She pulled some cash from her pocket.

"No you don't. It's on the house today."

"Are you sure?"

"Yes. Anyone who's working on the festival should stop in and grab some food. Don't worry about the line. We'll take care of our own first."

"Okay. I'm giving you a hug anyway." Kirsten wrapped an arm around Rose and gave her a quick squeeze before hurrying back to the ski shop where Amy, Sue and Bear were busy matching names to applications and bibs. A good number of people were also making purchases and renting skis and snowboards. Kirsten was elated. This was going to be a record day for them. She imagined the entire festival was going to bring in more in three days than they took in most of the year.

"Is everyone okay?" Kirsten asked.

"We're fine," Amy said.

"Aye." Bear nodded looking only a little overwhelmed, but then that smile of his lit up his face and she knew he was fine. The ladies in line were all vying to end up in front of him, but he seemed oblivious to it. There was something endearing about that. A man as handsome as Bear, who was completely unaware of what he did to women, or was he? The more she watched him, the more she doubted her original theory. He was very aware and he was using it to keep everyone in line smiling and laughing. She had to admit. The Scottish accent could melt the icy chill off of the most difficult customer.

Kirsten sat down next to Bear. "Rose says if you want anything to eat head on over. It's on the house today."

"I'll go in a few minutes," Amy said.

"I'll go after her." Sue handed the man in front of her his bib and instructions for the cross-country race the next day.

"Bear, you could go now if you want."

"Nae. I'll stay here."

"You can share my croissant and coffee with me." She broke off a piece of croissant and put it in his mouth as he opened it to speak. She couldn't help but giggle and neither could the woman standing in front of him.

"If he was mine, I'd make sure he was well fed, too." She took her bib and after one last lingering look at Bear, walked away fanning herself.

"You're good for business." Kirsten offered him the coffee, but he wasn't interested.

"Thank ye. I do me best."

"I can see that you do." She leaned closer to him, and spoke low so only he could hear. "I'm sorry about last night. I overreacted." She wasn't sure how he would receive her apology or if he'd hold a grudge. "Are we good?" she asked, watching his face as it relaxed a bit.

She jumped a little as his hand found her knee and squeezed. "Are ye asking me if I still like ye?" Bear had a teasing glint in his eyes.

"I guess I am."

He put his hand to his chin, pursed his lips and looked up and away. "Hmmm..."

"What does that mean?" she asked,

"It means I do." He leaned over and before she could stop him, kissed her. If she wasn't handing someone their bib and instructions, she was pretty sure she'd be kissing him back.

"Is it warm in here?" she asked.

"Not a bit," Sue said.

"Just checking." Turning to Bear she said, "We're going to have to have a little chat later about kissing the boss in front of the customers."

"Are ye planning to show me the correct way to do it?"

That took Kirsten completely off guard as she burst into laughter. "You're a wiseass."

By now everyone in line was in on their banter and seemed to be enjoying it as much as Bear.

She turned to address the crowd around her table, "Is everyone coming to the welcome bash tonight at the ranch?"

Several people nodded and said yes.

"What time does it start?" the woman standing in front of Bear asked.

"Seven. We've got some great entertainment planned. There will be good music, dancing and lots of good food and drink."

"I will be there."

"Are you staying at the inn?"

"Yes."

"I'm pretty sure they'll be shuttling guests back and forth to the party, so be sure and check with them."

"I will. Thanks."

After about another hour, there was a lull in the crowd. Amy was back and Sue was headed to Rose's for some food. "Can you handle things up front for a while?" Kirsten asked.

"Definitely," Amy answered.

"If you need us, yell."

"Of course."

Bear followed Kirsten back to the stock room. He was fairly certain that Kirsten didn't need his help, but if she wanted to talk to him about kissing he would go without complaint.

She closed the stock room door and turned to him. "I was thinking about you last night."

"All good thoughts?"

"It all depends on what you mean by good."

She approached him and he stayed perfectly still, not wanting to do anything that might stop her motion. He kept his arms at his side even though he wanted more than anything to pull her into his embrace. He shouldn't have worried though. She got right up close and wrapped her arms around his neck. "Now you can kiss me." She licked her lips in preparation and his cock stood at attention. She moved in closer. Their bodies were touching everywhere sending tingles from his head to his toes. Try as he might, he couldn't stop himself. He'd wanted to make her wait. To really want it. To really want him, but he couldn't hold out. One arm snaked around her back, his hand grasping her backside and nestling her up against him, wanting her to feel his hardness and desire for her. She gasped and then purred. His free hand tangled in her hair as he guided her lips towards his, teasing them with his tongue and as she opened for him, diving inside to fully explore the lips and mouth that had been teasing him all day. His hand left her hair, leaving a trail of tender caresses until he reached her breasts. Soft, full and trapped inside of some undergarment he was unfamiliar with. Nevertheless it only heightened his desire and hers it seemed.

"You are good," she said, pulling away to look into his eyes. "Very good."

"So I've been told," he teased.

"And so sure of yourself."

"Always."

"As much as I'd love to spend more time with you here among the boxes, I don't think this is the time or the place." They were both breathing hard.

"Yer correct as always." Bear continued to hold her body pressed against him.

"I'm glad you know who the boss is."

"Here in the store it would be ye." His eyes darkened with desire as he brushed her lips with his thumb. "In my bed, tonight, 'twill be me ye answer to."

Kirsten's eyes grew wide at that statement, but before she could respond Bear leaned in for another kiss and all thoughts left her.

The door to the storage room opened and Sue came in completely unaware they were there. When she saw them, she stopped dead in her tracks. "OMG! You two really need to get a room." She turned on her heel and left them.

Kirsten's voice was low and husky. "We should really get back out there. I want to go take one final look at the course for tomorrow before the party tonight. So, I'm going to go and I'll see you later."

"Later," he answered as he swatted her behind and watched her tantalizing backside sway to and fro as she left.

※

The Crooked Tails started playing at seven on the nose. The music greeting everyone as they entered the newly renovated barn was a mix of country and rock.

"This place looks great," Kirsten said. "You guys did an amazing job with it."

Cassie looked so proud. She'd created a winter wonderland. White trees filled with faerie lights were scattered throughout the large open space. Wide double doors were open allowing the guests to enter freely. Tables and chairs covered in shimmering white tablecloths and decorated with pine boughs and flowers surrounded a large dance floor. One wall held a buffet table filled with delectable delicacies that Rose had put together especially for this event. "We wanted a place where we could host receptions, banquets and parties."

"You've definitely done it."

Kirsten dressed in her sexiest outfit—a skin tight royal blue dress that accentuated her eyes—knowing it would make Bear crazy with wanting her. Not that he didn't already, but a little extra insurance was always good. He was across the room, greeting party guests and along with his brothers and Ross, completely rocking their kilts. Tonight, she was going to find out exactly what a Scotsman wore under his kilt and she couldn't wait. She blocked out everyone and everything around her as sensual thoughts of their earlier encounter ran through her head. She gripped the back of a chair to keep her knees from buckling out from under her.

"You look beautiful," Tim said, surprising her from behind and causing her to jump.

"Tim."

"It's me. In the flesh." His appreciative gaze traveled up and down her body. "Looks like the party's a success so far."

"Yes. Cassie and Ross did a great job," she said, reclaiming her personal space by moving a few steps away from him. She couldn't believe the nerve of him coming to stand so close that she could feel his hot breath on her neck.

"The races start tomorrow. You're working the downhill, right?" he asked as if nothing was wrong.

"That's right."

"Good. I'll be working alongside you," he announced as though she would be thrilled to hear it.

She turned her head so he couldn't read the disappointment on her face. The last thing she wanted to do was spend the day with Tim, but it didn't seem she had any choice. Bear and his brothers would be stationed along the cross-country course to help with any problems there.

"Would you like to dance?"

"Oh, no. I'm really supposed to be mingling with the guests. You know, making sure everyone's having a good time. If you'll excuse me." She began to walk away, but Tim grabbed her arm to stop her. She gazed down at his hand and he let go.

"I'm not a bad guy, Kirsten. I think you'd find me to be the perfect man for you if you'd only give me a chance."

"I really have to go." She hurried away from him, muttering to herself.

"What's wrong?" Cassie asked, intercepting her as she traveled to the farthest corner of the barn to avoid Tim.

"Nothing."

Cassie folded her arms, tipping her head and tapping her toe. "Don't give me that. I'm your best friend. I know when something's bothering you."

"You've got bigger things to concern yourself with right now. The party is a success by the way." Maybe if she changed the topic Cassie would drop her inquiry.

"Thanks, but that's not going to distract me. The look on your face is one I don't like. What happened?"

"Cassie, I think I'm falling for Bear."

"That's obvious, but not the problem."

Cassie knew something was up. She might as well tell her. "Tim's the problem. He won't give up. He calls me. Texts me and just now was trying to get me to dance with him while telling me what a good boyfriend he'd be." She wore her exasperation like a heavy cloak draped across her shoulders causing them to slump. She stared down at her feet feeling defeated.

"Your hands are shaking," Cassie said, taking hold of one and rubbing it. "Do you want me to ask him to leave?"

As great as that sounded, she knew it wasn't the right thing to do. "No. I have to work with the man, so I guess I can figure out how to avoid him here at the party."

"Are you sure?" Cassie asked.

"Yes. And please don't say anything to Ross or Bear," she pleaded.

Cassie hesitated and Kirsten could tell she was weighing the situation carefully before she spoke. "I won't."

"Promise?"

"Promise."

Their hug was spontaneous and exactly what Kirsten needed in the moment.

"Have you had anything to eat?" Cassie asked, guiding her towards the buffet tables.

"I haven't. I wasn't really hungry."

"You should eat."

Kirsten glanced around the room. Tim seemed to have vanished. Maybe he finally got the hint. Her mood lightened considerably. "Okay. Some food wouldn't hurt." Without Tim hounding her she'd be able to enjoy herself.

"This guy's really good," Kirsten said, referring to the singer and his band. "Where'd you find him?"

"Ross and I scouted out some of the bars in Truckee."

"Tough job."

"Very. Eventually we heard Jeff's band and he was the winner. Luckily he was available." Cassie glanced around the room. "I've got to go. Mingle, mingle, mingle," she ordered as she walked away.

"I will." Kirsten took a turn around the room greeting guests along the way and making sure everyone she spoke with was having a good time. She answered questions about the events that would be happening the next day, directed people to the restrooms and listened to a good number of people telling her how delighted they were to be in Delight. She didn't see Bear or his brothers anywhere. They were probably outside getting some fresh air. She decided to go take a look. The barn doors were wide open and as she approached she noticed a distinct change in temperature. She grabbed her coat from a hook by the doors. Peeking around some of the guests milling around the opening, she saw Bear and called to him.

Bear turned, "Kirsten!" A brilliant smile graced his normally serious face.

She pushed her way through the crowded doorway just in time to see a bright headlight aimed straight at Bear.

"Bear, look out!"

He turned and took a step towards her, but not in time to escape being sideswiped by a speeding snowmobile driven by someone completely dressed in black.

"Bear!" She ran to him. His brothers who had been standing nearby dropped to their knees to help him. "Bear! Are you okay? Kade, go get Ross." Kade did as he was told and disappeared into the barn. A crowd had formed around them.

Bear attempted to sit up, but Kirsten held him down. "Don't move." She immediately went into medic mode. "Does anyone have a light?"

"Why? I be fine," he protested trying to rise. She continued to hold him down and she was glad when he didn't fight her.

She was handed a flashlight and she used it to scan him for obvious injuries.

"Someone tried to run you down with a snowmobile," she said, hardly believing what she'd seen.

"'Tis good ye called to me. If ye had no' I fear they may have done more harm." He held Kirsten's hand and sat up.

"Did you hit your head?" She looked into his eyes, checking his pupils and their reaction to the light. Her professional demeanor was wearing thin and worry wasn't far behind. He could have been killed. The thought of it made her sick and it must have shown.

"No. Do no' fash, lass. I be fine." He touched her face, forcing her to focus her attention on his face. "I be fine."

He was okay, but she couldn't stop her hands from shaking.

Ross joined them. "Can ye stand?"

"I believe so."

Ross extended a hand to Bear, who grabbed on and between Ross pulling and Bear using him for leverage, he was able to get to his feet. His shirt was torn and there was blood running down his leg.

"He's bleeding," Kirsten said. "We should get him inside so we can take a better look at it.

Cassie joined them. "I thought you might need this," she said, handing Kirsten a towel.

The crowd made room for them to pass. They headed to the ranch house to tend to Bear and his injuries.

"Who was it?" Ross asked.

"I did no' see them," Payton said.

"Neither did I. All I could see was the headlight aimed right at Bear." Kirsten held tightly to Bear's hand, not wanting to let go.

"Do ye think they were trying to hit him on purpose?" Ross asked.

"I don't know, but it sure looked that way," she answered.

Once inside the house, Ross grabbed the supplies that Kirsten needed and then motioned to Payton.

"Come with me. We'll try tracking the snowmobile and see where it leads us."

Bear wasn't used to being fussed over, but since it was Kirsten doing the fussing he'd go along with it. He felt perfectly fine other than a gash in his leg which they'd already bandaged up and the unsettling feeling that he might just know who it was that tried to run him down.

"Are you going to be okay?" Cassie asked him.

"Aye. There's nae need for worry. I'll be fine. Kirsten has bandaged me up."

"Being a member of the ski patrol means I have to know how to deal with any injuries or illnesses we run across. It comes in handy."

He was seated on the sofa by the fire in the large living room of the ranch. Kade had returned to the party at Cassie's request. She wanted him to reassure the guests and tourists that everything was fine. Just an accident. They didn't want to scare everyone away the first day. "Are you sure you're okay?" she asked both he and Kirsten.

"Yes. We're fine. Go back to the party." Kirsten waved her hand towards the door where Cassie looked back one more time before disappearing out into the cold.

"I hope Ross finds who did this. He called the sheriff before he went out the door. He'll probably show up soon."

Bear hadn't had this much attention paid to him since he was a wee lad and even then his preference was to be left alone. If he had a choice, he'd much rather spend his time wooing Kirsten. The dress she wore left little to the imagination. It was short, tight and she wore it like a second skin. Her knees were a bit dirty from kneeling in the muck to take care of him, but he was sure he'd never seen a finer sight. Her attire puzzled him, as it hardly seemed practical and seemed more like something to be worn in the bedroom. The spiky heeled shoes in particular were impossible for him to ignore. If possible, they made her more enticing than she already was. He noted she'd had some difficulty walking in them as they sank into the muddied pathway that led to the ranch. He couldn't take his eyes off of her. Her honey blonde hair had fallen over one brilliant blue eye. Ruby red lips pouted prettily as she gently touched the area around his wound, causing his kilt to rise in response.

"What's going on there, mister?" she teased.

"I believe ye ken it since yer the cause."

"Am I?" she asked. The coy sound of her voice and the seductive glow darkening her eyes told him she was very aware of what she was doing to him.

"Come here." He hooked an arm around her neck and pulled her in so that their lips were almost touching. She nibbled on his lower lip as her hand found his male hardness beneath the kilt. A loud groan escaped his lips as he felt himself grow and become even harder with the touch of her silky soft hand. "I must have ye."

"Not here," she whispered in a low, sultry voice.

"Where then?" His cabin was close, but his brothers would join them before long.

"We'll go back to my place."

"I do no' believe I'll make it that far." He was ready to burst with wanting her.

"You'll have to." She teased him with a flick of her tongue across his lips. "I promise it will be worth it."

"I have nae doubt it will be. Let's go then." He began to rise from the sofa, but she pushed him back down.

"I think we should wait for the sheriff. He'll have questions."

"His questions can wait. We'll go now." He kissed her neck and down between her breasts.

Bear pushed himself up from the sofa and with one arm around Kirsten's waist, lifted her to her feet.

"I'll get my car. You wait here," she said.

"Nae. I'll no' let ye out of me sight."

"Are you sure you can walk that far?"

"I've a mere scratch on me leg. 'Tis no' enough to stop me from having ye, and the sooner the better."

"We've got all night." She leaned into him, kissing his mouth and playing at the crease with her tongue.

"We do, and I intend to show ye how to make use of every single moment."

CHAPTER 13

They spilled through the doorway to Kirsten's house, kissing, groping and tearing at each other's clothes. Kirsten had to admit it was much easier undressing Bear. That kilt was off in a flash and he was quite the feast for her eyes. She had to help him with her clothes. Holding her bra up by one finger, he looked at it as if it was the most fascinating thing he'd ever seen before flinging it across the room and almost hitting Kirby, who looked suitably bored and unimpressed with what was happening.

Kirsten took Bear's hand, leading him to her bedroom where she pulled him down onto the bed. They stared into each others eyes and then her hands went to work. She grasped his cock, enjoying the feel of his hardness and length. Bear's eyes closed as his head lolled back in ecstasy. Her body stretched up alongside his, small jolts of electricity passed between them in every spot where they touched. Bear's eyes opened and he looked at her with white hot lust.

"Do ye remember in yer store? I told ye I was the boss when I'd have ye in me bed."

"This isn't your bed." She nibbled on his ear, but it wasn't enough to distract him.

He expertly flipped her onto her back.

"Okay then," she laughed, enjoying the moment.

He lay atop her, kissing her lips, her eyes, her jaw, her neck, all the while holding her arms so she wasn't able to touch him. She bucked beneath him, unable to move in any other way. Her desire for him pulsed through her body creating powerful tremors of longing.

"What is it ye want, lass?" he asked.

"You." It was all she craved. Nothing more. Only Bear, any way he wanted.

His lips traveled from beneath her outstretched arm down her side and across her belly. She shivered in anticipation as his hands and mouth explored every inch of her. Kirsten closed her eyes, memorizing every touch, kiss and sensation that grew into an overwhelming ache to have him. She wasn't the type of woman who begged for anything, but this just might be her breaking point. She dug her nails into his back, wrapping her legs around him, urging him to the place she needed him to be before the practicalities of sex in the twenty-first century reared their head. "Wait."

"I do no' believe I can."

"You have to." She reached over to her end table and removed a condom, handing it to him.

"What's this?"

"Really, you have no idea what that is?" His puzzled expression told him he didn't have a clue and she couldn't wait any longer to have him inside of her. She ripped open the package, removing the condom. "This is to make sure that I don't get pregnant. There are other reasons, but I'm not going to get into that now, because I want you." she said as she placed it over his hardened cock. "Now, where were we?"

"I believe we were here," Bear answered, as his fingers explored her womanly folds.

"I like that," she said, a deep moan escaping her lips.

Bear smiled, teasing her a moment longer before entering her with a growl. They danced together in a rhythm that brought them both much pleasure. She stared into his eyes, not daring to look away for fear that this was all just a dream. His magnetic, dark gaze held hers with a strange magic she couldn't explain. All that mattered was this moment. They were both on the verge of climax, but held back wanting the passion they felt to last forever.

"I've wanted ye since the first time we met. I'd like it to last a while longer."

"I like the way you think."

Rolling onto his side Bear took Kirsten with him. They were perfectly in sync. Their bodies bending and flexing in concert with each other. He buried his face in her neck, inhaling her perfume as his tongue traveled up to her earlobe, which he gently nibbled, causing wild sensations to course through her body.

She pushed him onto his back and sat atop him moving to her own rhythm.

"Yer beautiful," he whispered. "Ye look like a goddess. My goddess."

Smiling down on her man, Kirsten writhed atop him. He grabbed her hips, guiding her until they were both moving frantically in search of satisfaction. As they reached their peak, Kirsten cried out and Bear called her name.

Exhausted and sated, they lay tangled in each other's arms unable to speak or move. It wasn't until some time had passed that they looked into each other's eyes and saw there that the spark they felt for each other had not been extinguished, but merely quenched for the moment.

"Did you eat anything at the party?" she asked, enjoying the feel of the man sharing her bed.

"I do no' believe so."

"I'll get us something to eat and be right back." She kissed his lips one more time before grabbing her robe and heading to the kitchen. On the way she checked her phone for messages. Cassie had texted her, so she texted back to let her know they were alright. Actually more than alright. She sent a quick message to the sheriff to let him know they'd speak with him in the morning and was just opening the refrigerator door when Bear came up behind her. He reached his hands inside her robe, running them across her belly and up to her breasts. She arched her back and leaned her head back into him.

"Yer the only food I need, lass." He turned her to face him and then lifted her onto the counter before entering her again. She wrapped her legs around his back and tangled her fingers in his hair. He held her face in his hands as he kissed her, probing her mouth with his tongue. The air around them was charged with an electric energy being generated by their two bodies coming together in perfect synchronized movements. The want and need they had for each other outweighed anything else. Mugs, dishes and a pitcher of milk were knocked out of the way as their passion grew, spiraling upwards to a peak that seemed just out of reach and then suddenly it wasn't. They reached their climax together and tumbled back down into each other's arms, out of breath, damp with sweat and happy.

"That was amazing!" Kirsten laughed.

"Aye, it was." Bear joined in her laughter.

They stared into each other's eyes. Bear gently kissed the corner of her mouth as it turned up in a satisfied smile.

"I think we made a mess," Kirsten noted, observing the spilled milk and one broken mug which had landed in the sink.

"It was worth it," Bear said. "Come, I'll help ye clean it up and then we can have that food you mentioned."

"I had forgotten all about it," Kirsten teased, playing with the hair on his chest.

"Do ye like that?" Bear asked with a mischievous glint in his eye.

"I do." She lifted one eyebrow. "And I like this, too." She swatted his naked bottom and tried to make a run for it, but he was too quick for her, grabbing her around the waist and pulling her into him. Her lips met his, igniting her passion again.

"Lass, ye've worn me out. I need a wee bit of time to recover."

"Boo," she pouted, pretending to be upset.

"It will no' take me long," he said, hurrying to appease her.

"Maybe some food will replenish your energy, but first the clean up." She grabbed a mop and some floor cleaner and made quick work of the milk. The mug in the sink was easy. She gathered the pieces and threw them in the trash.

While she did that, Bear stood with the door to the refrigerator open as he peered inside.

"See anything you like?" she asked.

Her turned to her with a wicked grin across his face.

"Remember, food first."

"Of course."

"Here, let me." He moved out of the way and Kirsten went to work grabbing cold cuts, cheese and pickles out of the refrigerator. She added bread and potato chips and then remembered mayo and mustard. "That should do it."

Bear watched as she expertly made them sandwiches and grabbed two cold bottles of beer. She put everything on a tray and brought it into the bedroom.

"Get back in bed," she ordered.

Bear did as he was told. She handed him the tray and she got in the bed beside him.

"Yer a good maker of sandwiches, lass."

"Thank you. I come from a long line of sandwich makers," she proudly stated.

"Are ye now?" His deep voice curled around her again, and she grinned back at him. He was so sexy, so fun to be with.

"Not really. Anyone can make a sandwich. It's pretty easy."

They finished the rest of the food and their beer.

Kirsten took the tray to the kitchen and when she returned, Bear was waiting for her.

"I'm ready, lass." He threw back the covers of the bed, inviting her to join him.

CHAPTER 14

"Today's going to be a good day," Kirsten crowed. Stretching her arms overhead, she sat up in bed next to the man she'd made love to for what seemed to be most of the night.

"The sun is barely up, lass. Come back here." He tried to pull her back down into his arms.

"I know and it's cold. I'd like nothing more than to curl up next to your warm body, but we can't." She hopped out of bed, running to grab her robe from a chair in the corner of the room. They hadn't taken the time to start a fire last night and the house was freezing. "We've got to get to the courses before anyone else." She shuffled into her slippers. "I'll get the shower started. Some hot water should make this a little easier."

Bear grimaced and pulled the blankets up to his chin. "If ye say so."

Kirsten started the shower, closing the door to capture the steam she knew would be filling the small space. Once it was ready, she peeked her head out the door. "I should go first."

Bear opened his eyes at that and the grin on his face was downright wicked, "I'll join ye."

"No, we'll never get out of here if you do." Why did she have to be so practical? She made a mental note to take him up on his offer later tonight or maybe tomorrow. Now that he'd put the thought in her head it was all she could do to maintain her focus and not change her mind.

"I do no' care for yer answer, but I'll abide by it because I ken yer right."

"Good. I won't be long and I'll try not to use up all the hot water."

"Please do no'."

Kirsten quickly showered and washed her hair. She brushed her teeth and threw her robe back on.

"Your turn."

Bear wasn't moving.

"Come on. We've got to be there early." She pulled the blankets off of him and he ran past her into the bathroom.

"I've become soft since I've been here. Heat and hot water have made me less of a man."

"I'll be the judge of that," Kirsten said. "You're all man as far as I'm concerned."

A long low moan erupted from Bear as he climbed in the shower. "'Tis heaven on earth."

"You'd think you didn't have heat and hot water back in Scotland." She thought about what Cassie had told her and wondered if it could possibly be true. She couldn't wrap her brain around it, so she wouldn't.

"We did no' have anything like this."

"That's crazy! You have to."

"Nae."

Maybe Cassie was telling the truth. Maybe they were time travelers. Once again, she shook that thought right out of her head. "I'm going to dry my hair and get dressed. We'll stop at the ranch so you can get some warmer clothes and pick up your brothers."

"Food?" he asked, sounding desperate.

"Yes. Food, too. I'm sure Cassie will feed us."

While she dried her hair, Kirsten replayed a few things in her head that seemed out of place besides the heat and hot water thing. She'd had to show him how to do almost everything at the store. He was unfamiliar with snowmobiles, certain foods, flashlights and any number of other things. This was starting to look more and more like some sort of strange dream. She wouldn't call it a nightmare because it involved Bear and he was definitely not a nightmare. She ran out to her truck and got the engine started to warm everything up before they got in. She brushed the snow off her windshield and then went back inside to hurry Bear along. To her surprise, he was ready and waiting for her.

"Shall we go?" he asked like she was the one holding things up. He breezed past her, giving her a peck on the cheek as he went.

"Okay then." She locked the door and got in the car, which was just starting to warm up. "I know I already asked you about this, but I find it hard to believe you don't drive." She pulled out of her driveway and onto the road that would take them to the ranch.

"Nae. We have none of these." He waved his hand back and forth in front of him.

"No cars? Or trucks?"

"No' a one," he answered.

For someone who came from a place where there were no cars or trucks, he certainly looked comfortable in this one.

"My feet and my horse have always gotten me where I needed to go."

"I'd like to see this place you call home. It sounds like it's lost in another time."

He glanced her way and Kirsten noted wide eyes and an open mouth. "Is something wrong?"

He made a grunting noise and gazed out the window.

She drove on and in a few minutes the ranch appeared on their left. She pulled in the driveway and got out, but Bear had beaten her to it. He was already at and through the front door.

"So much for being a gentleman," she muttered as she followed him in.

"I believe Kirsten suspects I'm from another time," Bear blurted out to Cassie and Ross. "What are we to do?"

"Tell her the truth," Cassie suggested.

Bear looked at Ross, hoping for a little more help than he'd just received.

"Cassie's right. Tell her."

He looked from one to the other. How could he tell her he was from a different time? How could he tell her he planned on going back as soon as he could figure out exactly how to do it.

"I prepped her a little for you," Cassie said. "She didn't believe me, but maybe she's ready to accept it."

"Someone was in quite the rush to get in here," Kirsten said, joining them in the kitchen. "He's hungry."

"Breakfast will be ready in no time. Ross is in charge of the pancakes and I'm getting the eggs together. Juice?"

"Yes, please," Kirsten answered.

"Can you get the pitcher out of the fridge and pour us all some?"

"Sure." Bear watched as Kirsten got four glasses and then a pitcher of juice from the cold box, as he called it.

"Coffee's already to go, too," Cassie said.

"Who wants a cup?" Kirsten asked.

"Pour some for everyone. Kade and Payton should be along any minute." The front door opened again. "And right on cue, here they are."

"Perfect timing," Kirsten said, pouring the coffee.

"I can smell food a mile away," Kade laughed.

Bear was happy to see that Kade was gaining back almost all of the weight he'd lost before their arrival. "Some things never change, do they lad?"

"Do we have enough plates and silverware out?" Kirsten wondered as everyone gathered around the kitchen eyeing the food.

"Six adults in the kitchen is pushing it, don't you think?" Cassie asked.

"Bear, where did ye go last night? Ye left us without so much as a goodbye." Kade had a teasing glint in his eye.

Bear snuck a peak a Kirsten, who's cheeks reddened just a bit. She lifted her eyes and caught him looking. The two shared silly grins that seemed duly noted by the others. "I went home with Kirsten."

"I wanted to keep an eye on him," she added.

The others all had a good chuckle over that.

"Well, I did," Kirsten said, sounding a bit indignant.

"What did the sheriff have to say last night?" Bear asked.

"He was surprised, but attributed it to someone who probably had a little too much to drink and not much experience with a snowmobile. Ross and Payton found it further out on the property abandoned in a ditch."

"So you don't think it was on purpose?" Kirsten asked, sounding worried.

Ross and Bear exchanged a knowing look. They both had their suspicions, but they wouldn't voice them here.

"It seemed odd to me, but the sheriff was convinced of his theory." Cassie put the eggs out on the counter and Ross plated the pancakes. Everyone grabbed a stool at the oversized counter and started filling their plates. "How are you feeling today, Bear?"

"Better than I've ever felt." He snuck a glance in Kirsten's direction and her lips curved upwards in a smile meant just for him.

"No harm done then," Cassie said.

Eggs and bacon were passed from one to the other until everyone's plates were filled.

"You've got quite the appetite this morning," Cassie teased, raising an eyebrow at Bear and Kirsten.

Kirsten's cheeks pinked up a bit more. "We've got a big day ahead of us. We need the calories."

"Sure. Sounds about right," she winked.

"It's true," Kirsten protested.

"We believe you, don't we Ross?"

"Aye." Ross didn't seem too interested in anything more than eating.

"Can we stop dancing around what you are obviously getting at?" Kirsten's irritation at her friend's teasing was showing.

"I don't know what you're talking about." Cassie held one hand up to her chest pretending innocence.

Bear chuckled to himself. "The food is quite good this morning."

"Are you saying it's not always this good?" Cassie asked.

"'Tis always good. This morning it seems even better than usual." A lopsided grin was sent Kirsten's way.

Kirsten finished the last of her coffee. "I've got to get going. Bear do you know where you're going and can you show Kade and Payton what needs to be done?"

"Aye."

"Ross. You're in charge of getting everyone started."

"Aye."

"I'll see you all later then." Kirsten bolted out the door.

"She's full of energy this morning," Cassie noted.

Bear smiled. Their little secret wasn't so secret anymore.

Kirsten wasn't looking forward to her encounter with Tim, but she might as well get it over with. They had to work together today and it was better if it wasn't awkward.

"Hey, Tim." She said, entering the office where the ski patrol were all gathered awaiting their orders for the day. Tim handed out the schedule and everyone got their equipment together and headed for the lifts.

"You and I are taking the racecourse today," he replied, his voice flat and lacking emotion.

"Hopefully it'll be uneventful." That was the goal for the day as far as Kirsten was concerned. No accidents and no drama.

"We'll see." Tim didn't seem to have a lot to say today. Things were feeling a bit awkward between them.

"Did you hear what happened last night at the party?" she asked, wondering where he'd gone off to and if he was still present when Bear was run down.

"No. I left early. I knew we were going to have a big day today and I wanted to get a good night's sleep. Tell me about it." Despite what he was saying, the disinterest in his voice was obvious.

"Someone tried to run Bear down with a snowmobile." Kirsten watched him carefully as their conversation continued.

"Really. Why would anyone do that?" He shuffled through some papers on his desk, never once looking up at her.

"I don't know. They didn't catch them though."

"Any clues as to who it might be?"

"Not really. They ditched the snowmobile in a ditch. Ross said it was one of theirs. Someone took it without them knowing. Luckily it wasn't damaged."

"Good thing. They can be expensive to repair."

"The sheriff thinks it was someone from the party who had a little too much to drink."

"They called the sheriff?" For the first time, Tim looked up and showed an interest in what she was saying.

"Of course. Why wouldn't they?"

"I guess that makes sense either way." He went back to his paper shuffling.

Kirsten was feeling irritated with him. "I'd say so. Someone stole their snowmobile, almost ran down Bear and could have possibly been driving drunk."

"You said almost ran Bear down. He wasn't hurt then?"

"Just a cut on his leg. We patched him up and he's as good as new."

Tim seemed disappointed to hear this. "We should get going. The racers will be heading up the slopes in the next few minutes. We don't want to be late." He held the door open for her as she passed.

"Everything's ready in case of an injury?" she asked, breezing by him.

"Snowmobiles stationed along the route. First aid kits. Radios for communication. EMTs ready and waiting. I think we're all set."

"Okay. Let's go then." She began walking away, but found Tim right beside her.

"Kirsten, I don't mean to be a pain. I know I've been getting on your nerves lately and I wanted to apologize," he said, with true sincerity in his voice.

Kirsten was taken aback by this change in his demeanor. "That means a lot. I appreciate it."

"I realize we have to work together and I didn't want to make that difficult."

"We're on the same page then," she said. She headed towards the ski lifts, but Tim stopped her again.

"Yeah. There is one thing I did want to say." He had his hand on her arm. She glanced down at it and he removed it, adjusting his goggles atop his head.

Kirsten tried to keep the irritation off of her face. For a brief moment there she thought maybe, just maybe she'd gotten through to him. She braced herself for what he might have to say. "Okay. What is it?"

"I'll say it and then I'll never bring it up again. I promise."

Her patience was wearing thin. "Yes," her voice was tight as she tipped her head waiting for his reply.

"This guy, Bear. Be careful around him. There's something about him that worries me. I can't quite put my finger on it, but I know he's really into you and I'm just worried that he's one of those obsessive jealous types."

She could see why he might project his own faults onto Bear. But it wasn't Bear that was being weird and obsessive. "Don't worry. I've got it under control, but thanks. I appreciate your concern." There, perhaps they could have a normal, friendly relationship now that he'd said his piece.

They left the office and took a chairlift up to the top of the race course. Once there, they each went to their designated area on the course. With ski patrol stationed every fifty feet or so they should be fine if there were any accidents. Snow flurries were still coming down, but visibility was pretty good. Hopefully, the heavy snow that had been forecasted would wait until later that night to fall.

On the cross-country course, Bear, his brothers and some of the townsfolk were stationed along the route. They were there to handle any emergencies that might crop up, to hand out water and to make sure the skiers stayed on course. As with the downhill races, this was a mix of pros and amateurs trying their hand at racing for the first time.

Bear was fascinated with all of the equipment that the skiers used, as well as the radio he'd been handed. Ross gave him and his brothers a brief lesson in their use and they'd been having fun with it ever since.

"Bear," Kade's voice came through the radio. "'Tis me."

"I ken 'tis ye."

Silence. Bear chuckled to himself. His youngest brother had really taken to life here in this time. He was fascinated by all of the things they saw, heard and tasted.

"I'm back. I forgot to press the button as Ross explained to me."

"I thought so. We should save the radio for emergencies, Kade."

"Aye. 'Tis what Ross told me. I'll go now. Over and out."

Again, Bear chuckled at his brother. It was good to see him happy and well fed. He hadn't thought Kade would make it the day of the avalanche. He'd been starving and exhausted. If it wasn't for the time travel, Kade would probably be dead. That gave Bear pause. The thought of losing either of his brothers tore at his heart. He was grateful they were safe, but he couldn't help but bemoan the loss of the life he'd once had. The life he wished to have again. If the opportunity arose for him to return, he had no doubt he would do it in an instant. His chest tightened uncomfortably at that thought and a vision of Kirsten smiling at him crossed his mind.

At that moment, he was distracted as a group of skiers made their way by him and unlike those who'd passed first, these people were slower and more friendly, waving and shouting at him as they started their way up the hill in front of them. A few stopped briefly, groaning at the sight, but then gamely began their trek. It took a while before they were at the top and then out of sight.

"Last group of skiers are on the course," was barked through the radio.

"Aye," he barked back.

The woods around him were quiet. Something about the fallen snow muffled the normal sounds making everything peaceful and serene. It would be a few minutes before the skiers reached him and then he would trudge back down to the starting line to wait. He hoped Kirsten was enjoying the day as much as he was. The fact that she was working with Tim didn't sit well with him, but she'd made it clear that he should mind his own business and Bear would do as she wished.

The sounds of winded skiers reached his ears. He peered through the trees and caught a glimpse of bright red, blue and yellow heading his way. There seemed to be three of them. Bear was at the midpoint in the race. The racers would pass him, head up hill and once at the top be on flat ground again until it was time to head downhill to the finish line.

As they approached him, huffing and puffing, they hesitated only briefly before starting their climb. He watched until they'd made it to the top and were out of sight before turning to head back to the starting line. He stopped as he saw one more skier headed his way. They seemed to be struggling more than the others and she stopped in front of him, gasping for breath.

"Do ye need help, lass?" he asked.

"I don't think I can do this," she said. "The hill."

"'Tis the hardest part. Once ye've made it to the top 'twill be easy. Ye'll see." Despite his encouraging words, Bear was worried she wouldn't be able to make it.

The woman didn't answer him. Instead she stood staring at the hill as if it were the face of a mountain.

"Do ye wish to go back?" he asked.

"I have to do it. I told my husband and children I was going to do it."

"Perhaps if I go with ye," he suggested.

"Would you?" She turned desperate eyes in his direction.

"I would." He moved to stand beside her. "I can no' help ye. 'Tis against the rules."

"Just knowing I'm not alone would mean the world to me," she said.

"All right then." Bear moved in front of her. "Follow me."

He started uphill in his snowshoes and the woman followed. He checked back behind him, stopping occasionally and waiting for her to catch up.

"I'm afraid I'm going to slide backwards," she admitted.

"I'll get behind ye then. I won't let ye slide."

A grateful smile lit her face as she slowly made her way by him. "What's your name?"

"Bear, and yers?"

"Emily."

"Yer almost to the top, Emily. Yer family will be proud of ye."

"I'll be proud of me," she said.

Once at the top, they stopped to let her catch her breath before continuing on. They passed Kade, who followed them and then Payton, who did the same. As they got closer to the finish line, Bear motioned for them to stop.

"Emily, yer on yer own now. Go on. Ye can do it."

"Thank you, Bear."

She cruised the rest of the way downhill, making it to the finish line, where Bear watched her be engulfed by her family.

"Come," he said to his brothers.

The snow was starting to fall harder now. It was good that the race was over. At the finish line, he congratulated Emily and greeted her family before checking in with Ross and Cassie.

"That's it," Cassie said. "She was the last skier."

"Let's go home," Ross said. "'Tis time for something to warm our insides."

"See you at the gathering tonight," Cassie called to the few remaining stragglers at the finish line.

"I wonder how things are going with the downhill," Ross said.

"Hopefully as good as they went here. I think it was a huge success. Thank you guys," she said to Bear, Kade and Payton.

"We were happy to help," Kade answered.

They made it back to the ranch in record time, passing the field that held the snowman building competition, which was still going on. When they reached the house, Amy was waiting for them. "I got a fire going for you and I heated up some hot chocolate."

Bear noted that the men seemed disappointed. No doubt they would prefer something stronger.

"You should see your faces." Amy laughed. "I may have accidentally put a dash of whisky in it."

"Och, Amy," Kade pulled her in for a hug. "Thank ye."

A joyful smile spread across Amy's now pink-tinged face. "You know, if I was ten years younger, I could really go for you," she teased.

"Do no' let that stop ye," Kade replied, still holding onto her.

"It goes against my no-robbing-the-cradle ethos."

"I didn't know you had one of those," Cassie said, rolling her eyes skyward.

"Shush, you!" Amy said, disconnecting herself from Kade and grabbing some mugs for the hot chocolate. "This is my secret recipe," she whispered, handing drinks to everyone.

They all crowded around the fire, warming themselves and sipping their hot chocolate.

"Things are going well at the downhill venue," Amy said. "Kirsten checked in with me just before you got here. They were almost done and then she'll be on her way here."

CHAPTER 15

"*I* missed you," Kirsten said, falling into Bear's arms the moment the others were out of sight.

"Ye've been on my mind all day." He replied before capturing her lips in a hungry kiss. "I want nothing more than to return to yer bed. Shall we go now?"

"I'm afraid we can't."

Kirsten held back her laughter as she watched the sad disappointment spreading across Bear's face.

"Why?"

"We have to attend the party tonight. They're giving out the ribbons for the winners of today's races and other events. Besides, I've been planning this thing with Cassie for months. I'm not going to miss a second of it. A few more days and it'll be done until next year. We can spend the next week in bed, if that's what you want."

"Aye." He pulled her close, capturing her lips once again.

Kirsten felt all off-kilter. His kisses were potent magic. The more she thought about it, the more she thought that a week in bed might be the best idea she'd ever had. "Let's go see what everyone else is doing."

"No' a thing more important that this," he said refusing to let her go and impressing his want upon her with a rock hard cock she could feel through all her layers of clothes.

"It's getting hot in here." She pulled off her scarf and unzipped her jacket.

"I can help ye with that," Bear said, the look of a ravenous wolf in his eyes.

"You do know that there are people in the next room, don't you?"

"I do."

"And you don't care?"

"No' at all."

"You're incorrigible!" She wriggled away from him, throwing all of her outer layers on the sofa in Cassie's office.

"That is good, aye?"

"Sometimes."

Before he could grab hold of her again and work his magic on breaking down her defenses, she hurried out the door and into the living room apparently looking quite flushed.

"You okay?" Cassie asked, giving her the once over.

"I'm fine. Why?"

"You look a little overheated, if you know what I mean."

Bear joined them, revealing nothing. "Aye. She needed to remove her clothes."

"Not my clothes, Bear. My jacket and scarf. That's all." The others were eyeing her with smug grins. "Know-it-alls!"

"I'll get you some hot chocolate," Amy said, and then over her shoulder as she walked away, "I can throw some ice into it if you're still too hot."

Everyone snickered. Kirsten's deadly glare told them she wasn't amused.

Amy returned, handing her the cocoa.

"Mmm... Delicious." Kirsten took another sip of Amy's famous hot chocolate. "How much time do we have before this evenings festivities?"

"Another hour or so."

"I was hoping to get some time for a nap." The disappointment on her face and in her voice were obvious.

"You can do that. We've got everything set up. The only thing we need to do is get the bonfire started and make sure our evening's entertainment gets set up. If you're a few minutes late getting back it's fine."

"No. I'll stay here and help. Once this is over I'll have plenty of time for napping."

"Are you sure?" Cassie asked.

"Positive. I'll get my second wind and I'll be good to go."

"We're going to go gather the course markers," Ross said. "We'll be back before long." He gave Cassie a quick peck on the lips.

"Ladies, shall we hit the barn and make sure everything is ready?"

"Let's go." Kirsten grabbed her jacket and followed Cassie and Amy.

They checked the buffet station where Rose was already setting everything in place on the long tables. The band was doing a mic check. Cassie handed Kirsten programs to set out on each of the tables. When they were finished they all gathered together for a group hug.

Bear headed back to his cabin with Kade and Payton. They'd helped Ross remove the course markers and now they had a short while to rest and get ready for the evening. It had been a long day and they'd spent most of it outdoors. Bear was becoming spoiled by the warmth of their cabin, hot water and the ability to cook without having to start a fire.

Kade immediately dove onto the sofa. "Ahhh... How lucky are we to be here in this time?"

Payton retired to his bed, leaving Bear to deal with Kade.

"Do ye no' think 'tis wrong that we have so many luxuries when our fellow Highlanders suffer so in our own time?" Bear asked.

"No." He propped his head on a pillow and closed his eyes. "Ye should rest brother."

Shaking his head, Bear walked into the bedroom to his bunk. He climbed into his bunk wondering if it would make him a bad chieftain if he were to stay here instead of going back home. Was it even possible to return? He'd done much to occupy his mind so he wouldn't think too much on it. He was torn. He wanted to stay here with Kirsten, but he wanted to go home so that he could retrieve the life he'd once lived. He needed to save his people, but could he?

He closed his eyes, trying to block those thoughts out. It didn't work. All he could see were the people he counted as friends eating what little scraps they could find, looking thinner and thinner and having nothing they could call their own. His gut boiled with anger at their misfortune and his inability to save them.

As Ross had told him, if he went back it would only be a matter of time before he was arrested and either hung or sent off to the colonies as slave labor. Why go back? He was already in what was once the colonies, but not as a prisoner. Why this had happened was baffling, but should he question whatever power had saved them from the fate that would have surely befallen them?

"I can no' rest," he said out loud.

Payton sat up and gazed at him with a sadness that was palpable.

"I close my eyes and I see those we've left behind," Bear admitted.

"Brother, I understand."

Bear was the one who should understand, but how could he. He'd never suffered such a loss like the one Payton had endured. Every day he watched as his brother somehow managed to do all of the things he must. It tore at his heart to watch Payton suffer. He wished he could somehow make Payton's pain his own. That he could lift the heavy burden of sorrow from Payton and carry it himself. "I'm sorry Payton. Ye've yer own sorrow to tend to."

"Sleep does no' come easy for me. I see my wife and our bairn in every dream. It's so real to me. I can feel them when I hold them in my arms. I hear her voice calling to me and I hear the bairn cry out to me. When I wake I remember they are gone and I could no' save them."

"Do ye wish to go back home?"

"It does no' matter to me whether I be here or there. My life will never be the same. I'm with ye and Kade and yet I be alone."

Bear's heart hurt for his brother. There was nothing he could do to ease his pain. It seemed there was little he could do for anyone, even himself.

❄

"Hey, are you okay?" Kirsten asked when Bear arrived for the evening's festivities. She wrapped an arm around his waist and placed a comforting hand on his chest. He seemed sad about something and she wanted to be there for him. He glanced down at her and it was clear to her. "What's wrong? And don't tell me nothing."

"I've much on my mind. I worry about my brother."

"Payton or Kade?"

"Payton. His wife and bairn have passed and his grief weighs on him."

She gasped on hearing this. "I'm so sorry. I didn't know."

"'Tis why he does no' speak much."

"Understandable after suffering such a terrible loss. How did it happen?" she asked.

"The fever took them."

Kirsten pulled back a bit to see his face. That was an odd thing to say.

"I want to help him, but I do no' ken what to do."

"I imagine just being there for him. Listening when he wants to talk."

She could feel the defeat he was wearing like a heavy cloak. It was so unlike him. He was her strong, brave Highlander and it seemed that at this moment he needed her strength and counsel.

"Where is he? Is he coming tonight?"

"Nae. He wishes to be alone."

"You're such a good big brother to be so worried about him."

"I can no' help him."

Kirsten took his hand and they walked around the space in silence. She had no idea what she could say that would help. She leaned into him, resting her head on his upper arm as they walked. They headed to the two large doors that would lead them out of the barn and down a path to a wooden bench where they could sit and look at the lights. She knew Bear loved them. She did too. There was something about them that made everything seem more peaceful and bright. They sat quietly for a long time before Kirsten spoke again. She hoped her words would bring some solace to this man she cared so much about.

"Everyone grieves in their own way. It might take him longer than you'd like, but some day you'll see the light at the end of the tunnel. Some day he'll wake up and take a tiny step away from the grief. In the meantime, all you can do is try to keep him from going backwards."

"Aye. Yer right. Thank ye, lass. Those were the words I needed to hear."

"I'm happy to help. Shall we walk a little bit more?"

Bear stood, taking her hand again and they walked further down the path, enjoying the brisk night air and searching for stars in the deep blue pockets of sky visible between the clouds.

"When I was a little girl, we'd go camping in my parents RV to look for shooting stars."

"What's an RV?" he asked.

"A motorhome, like a camper." They must call them something different in Scotland.

He nodded his head, saying "I see." Kirsten wasn't sure he did.

They circled back to the barn where the party was in full swing.

"What can I do to make you smile?" Kirsten asked as she poked him in the ribs.

His face softened as his lips twitched upward.

"There, that's better. Now, I want you to dance with me before we get so busy around here that we won't have time."

"I do no' ken yer dances," he said, glancing around at the people hopping around the dance floor.

"Really? You don't dance?"

170

He scrunched his brows together and shook his head.

"Come on. They're playing a slow song now." She took him by the hand and dragged him out to the middle of the floor. Kirsten placed his hands on her waist and she wrapped her arms around his neck. "Like this."

Bear moved his hands around to her lower back, pulling her closer.

"You can do this, right?"

"Aye."

"Now, move along with me to the music." Kirsten was pleased. Considering that he had no idea what he was doing, he was a pretty good dancer. This was nice. Strong arms held her close to a rock hard chest. Gazing up into dark chocolate eyes, she felt a connection with him. The connection. The one she'd been searching for, but felt she might never find. There was something more to this man. Something that had been becoming more and more apparent to her the longer she knew him. She had to know the truth. "Bear, can I ask you a question?"

"Ye can."

"Cassie told me that you are a time traveler. Is that true? Or was she pulling my leg?"

He stopped moving as a loud sigh escaped his lips. "'Tis true."

"How did you get here?" Kirsten asked, prodding him to start dancing again.

"The avalanche."

"It brought you here? All the way from Scotland?"

"We were caught in an avalanche on Ben Macdhui, 'tis a mountain in the Highlands. The Old Grey Man may or may not have had something to do with it. When we came out of it, we were here."

"Who's the grey man?"

"He lives on the mountain. I always thought it was only a legend, but after all we've been through, I can no' deny his existence."

"Is he like bigfoot?"

"I do no' ken who that is."

Kirsten laughed. "It doesn't matter. I'm still trying to wrap my head around the fact that you're from a different time."

"1747."

"Wow." That would explain a lot. "This goes against everything I believe to be true. I thought time travel was something you only found in novels and movies."

He appeared confused, which only confirmed what he'd been telling her. This was not something he was making up. This was something he was living. How strange this all must seem to him. Her protective instincts kicked in. "Don't worry. I won't tell anyone and you shouldn't either."

"I have no' told a soul."

"Good." She rested her head on his chest as they continued swaying in place to the music. She was happy here in his arms, happier than she'd been in a very long time. A sudden thought occurred to her. What if she lost him? It was painful to think about and so she simply had to ask. "Are you going to go back? Can you go back?"

"I do no' wish to leave ye, but there are many responsibilities I have. There are those who depend on me."

She didn't like the sound of that. "I don't want you to leave."

"I do no' ken how I could. Another avalanche perhaps."

"That sounds much too dangerous. What if it didn't work? You'd be buried alive." The thought terrified her.

"I do no' wish to think on it now. I wish to hold ye in me arms and enjoy the warmth of your body."

How could she argue with that? She had so many questions, but they could wait. They had time. She was sure of it.

"Two down. Two to go." Cassie turned off the lights in the barn and closed the doors.

They stood around under the large outdoor light that

hung above the barn doors. Snow fell in large soft flakes, landing on their heads and shoulders.

"We've been lucky with the snow so far," Kirsten observed, holding up her mittened hands and catching some of the rare beauty in the palms of her hands.

"I don't know how long our luck will last. There were a few times over the last twenty-four hours when I thought we were in trouble, but then the snow backed off a bit."

"From what I've seen on the weather reports, we should be okay tomorrow. The last day of the festival will definitely be impacted by a huge snowfall that's expected tomorrow night."

"Hopefully people stick it out and don't go home early."

"No matter what happens, the festival has been a huge success."

"Are we going to make it an annual event?"

"Definitely. I've got lots of plans for other events through the year, but this has been a winner."

"Good night everyone." Amy waved as she headed to her car.

Kade tagged along beside her. "I'll walk ye to yer car."

Kirsten had to laugh. Kade had taken a liking to Amy and she felt the same about him. It wasn't a romantic relationship, but more like a brother and sister. The two were a constant source of amusement as they teased and played jokes on one another.

The others took their cue from Amy and followed along behind her.

"Do you guys want to come to the ranch for a night cap?" Cassie asked, glancing at Ross who didn't seem quite as interested in entertaining as she did.

"I think I'll head home," Kirsten said, gazing up at Bear. "You want to come with?"

Bear's soft smile warmed Kirsten. She took his hand and they began the walk to her car. "Good night," she called back over her shoulder. "I can't wait to get home. I'm exhausted."

"Kirby will be happy to have ye home."

"Maybe. He's pretty independent."

The drive home was filled with comfortable small talk. Nothing more was said about time travel. Not that Kirsten was done asking about it, but she wanted to be wide awake the next time the subject came up.

Bear reached across the front seat, caressing her cheek with his thumb. It all felt like perfection to Kirsten. He was everything she'd hoped for, wanted and needed. Now that he was here she couldn't imagine what her life would be like if he left.

Once in the driveway, Bear got out and came around to open her door. She stepped out and after closing the door stumbled into him. Her muscles were sore from a long day on the slopes, not to mention the previous evening's activities. She'd been on her feet all day and throughout the evening party. She grabbed onto his arm, but Bear had other ideas. He lifted her into his arms and carried her to the house. She didn't resist. It was okay to let someone take care of her, especially since that someone was Bear. She wrapped her arms around his neck as he made his way to her bed, gently depositing her there. He carefully removed her clothing, one layer at a time and then tucked her in under the covers.

"Are you going to join me?" she asked.

"I'll be back," he replied, leaving the room.

Kirby was weaving himself in and out of Bear's legs. "Are ye hungry?" Bear asked.

"His food is in the kitchen," Kirsten called.

"I remember," Bear called back to her.

She could hear him speaking softly to the cat. The sounds of water running and the tea kettle being placed on the stove told her what he was doing. She closed her eyes, enjoying how it felt to allow herself to sink into the pillow and mattress. Bear returned with two mugs of tea, placing them on the nightstand before undressing and getting into bed beside her. She propped herself up on the pillows.

"You're a very special man," she said to him. "I didn't realize until now how much I hate being alone. I've done it for so long that it became normal to me. Having you here with me, making me tea and taking care of me... I know I don't want to be alone anymore."

He leaned over and kissed her gently on the lips. "As long as I be here in this time, ye will no' be."

"Does that mean you're going to leave?"

"I can no' say. 'Twould be hard to leave ye. I do no' ken that I could."

So, things were a little up in the air between them. She sipped her tea before setting it on the end table and crawling into Bear's arms. She rested her head on his chest, listening to the strong, steady beat of his heart. He was a living, breathing man and he was here beside her. She had to believe he would stay and that what they had would continue to grow, strengthening into the love she'd always wished for. She closed her eyes and allowed the beat of his heart to lull her to sleep.

CHAPTER 16

*I*ce sculpting, snowshoeing and snowboards were the events of the day and like the previous day, everything was going smoothly. Participants were thrilled with everything and so were the residents of Delight.

Payton was out early feeding and caring for the horses. Bear joined him and when they were done, they saddled up four of the horses. Each Highlander would ride one today. Bear, along with Evie, would be stationed at the snowshoe course. Ross was to be at the foot of the slopes where the snowboard competition was to be held. Kade and Payton would be at the ranch overseeing the ice sculpting and taking photos with visitors. They, of course, all wore their own kilts along with long johns to keep them warm under their period clothing. They looked amazing and guests at the ranch were loving it.

Rose and Walt arrived and set up a booth with coffee, hot chocolate, tea and enough baked goods to feed an army of visitors. It was the final day of competitions and everything was going as planned.

Kirsten was on the slopes. She was thankful Tim had found something else to occupy himself. She was so much more relaxed knowing she wasn't going to have to deal with him today.

There were more than a few wipeouts on the slopes but nothing serious enough to require medical attention, leaving Kirsten and the other volunteers able to relax and enjoy the skill of the competitors.

At the noon break, everyone headed to the lodge for lunch. Kirsten decided to drive over to the snowshoe venue and see how Bear was doing. She hadn't had a chance to see him on horseback because she'd had to leave before they were saddled up. She was excited to see him as he looked back in his own time.

Pulling in at the ranch, she hurried past the ice sculpting, admiring Kade and Payton's authenticity. She waved to them and they waved back. They seemed to have a line of people waiting to take photos with them. Kade, of course, was beaming. Payton on the other hand remained serious.

As she approached the snowshoers, she heard a crack. Growing up here in the mountains, she knew a gunshot when she heard one and that was a gunshot. She began to run as another shot rang out. A few of the snowshoers waiting for their turn on the course, glanced around, but surprisingly no one else seemed phased by it. There was so much activity and noise from the crowds that it was possible the sound got lost in the din. She spotted Bear up ahead at a bend of the trail. It had been his job to keep the racers on course, but at the moment he was busy trying to calm Evie who had obviously been spooked by the shot. She could see him twisting this way and that in the saddle, peering into the woods behind him. Bear hardly seemed phased as he guided Evie away from the crowds of onlookers. He spoke softly, stroking her neck with the reins until she calmed.

"Are you okay?" Kirsten asked, running up to them.

"Stay there," Bear ordered. "I do no' wish ye to be hurt."

"Oh, sorry." She moved back away.

Bear turned Evie in a circle until she calmed and then he trotted her over to Kirsten.

"What happened?" she asked. "I thought I heard gunshots."

"Ye did."

"Was someone shooting at you?" she asked, trying to keep the panic out of her voice.

"I do no' believe so. If they were, they need practice."

"Don't joke about that. You could have been killed."

"I was no'. All is well. Evie was spooked, but now she is fine. She's no' used to such things."

"Neither am I. Come down here. I need to hug you."

"As ye wish." He hopped down from Evie, who stayed close by his side. "Come, lass. All is well." He held out his arms to her and she fell into them.

"This is crazy. Are you sure you're okay?" She pulled away and looked him over from head to toe.

"Are there any holes in me?" he chuckled.

"No and this isn't funny."

"Come. Ride with me. I'm bringing Evie back to the barn. She has had enough for today."

He lifted her up into the saddle and hopped up behind her. Kirsten couldn't help but feel that this might be the single most romantic thing that had ever happened to her. Unfortunately, it was ruined by the fear that had gripped her.

At the barn, Bear set Kirsten on the ground then unsaddled Evie and put her in her stall. He gave her a flake of hay and then brushed her coat and combed out her mane and tail.

Kirsten was impressed with the gentle way he handled the mare. It was apparent that Evie loved and trusted him. She thought she and Evie might have something in common.

"I'm calling over to the snowboard course to tell them I'm not coming back. If they need me I can get there in no time."

As they were leaving the barn, Ross rode up on his horse. "Are ye done for the day?"

"Aye."

"Ross, did you hear gunshots?" Kirsten asked.

"Nae. I didnae. What happened?" He exchanged a look with Bear before dismounting. "Come talk with me while I put Galaxy away." He walked down the barn aisle to an empty stall.

Kirsten explained what she thought had happened as Ross unsaddled his horse and did a bit of grooming.

"I've nae heard anyone say a thing about it." Ross gave Galaxy a carrot and he happily chomped away at it.

"How can we find out?" Kirsten asked.

"I don't know, but we better call the Sheriff."

"I don't think he's been this busy in forever," Kirsten said.

"I'll meet ye inside," Ross said. "I'm just going to finish up here."

Bear and Kirsten headed inside. The ice sculpting contest was wrapping up and Kade and Payton were headed back to the barn as well.

"Cassie!" Kirsten called as they came in.

"I'm in my office," Cassie answered.

Kirsten peeked her head inside the door. "We need to call the sheriff."

"What? Are you kidding me?" Cassie jumped up out of her chair. "What happened now?"

"I think someone was firing at Bear."

Cassie had the phone to her ear. "Sheriff, it's Cassie. We need you at the ranch." She listened for a minute before speaking again. "Kirsten thinks someone shot at Bear on the snowshoe track. Okay. Bye."

"What did he say?"

"He's heading over there and he'll see if anyone knows anything. No one else has called in about shots fired, so it might be hard to figure out. He's on it though."

K irsten couldn't sleep. She was up pacing back and forth in her living room. Bear was sound asleep in her bed. She should be there with him, but she couldn't turn her brain off. She thought about the gun shots. Had she been hearing things? No. Bear and Evie both heard it. Who would do something like that? Her thoughts immediately went to Tim. Was he capable of doing something like that? He was probably busy on the slopes. Maybe she could ask a team member to confirm his whereabouts. That would have to wait though. It was the middle of the night. No one was going to appreciate her waking them up at this hour.

She wandered back into the bedroom and looked at Bear. Kirsten had fallen hard for the handsome Highlander. She'd never felt this way about anyone and wanted to see where this relationship could go, but would she have that chance? A chill came over her and she briskly rubbed her arms. What if Bear had been hit? He might be gone. He might leave anyway she reminded herself. There were no guarantees in life.

She looked at Bear sleeping so peacefully in her bed and decided to climb back in and hold him close for as long as she could.

CHAPTER 17

Kirsten woke with a start at the sound of the alert on her cell phone. Her Search and Rescue app was set up to notify her of any emergency situations so she could respond quickly. She hopped from bed and grabbed her phone, turning the alert off and reading the message she'd received.

"What horrible sound is this?" Bear asked rolling over and searching for Kirsten.

"It's an alert from the mountain. There's a missing skier. I've got to go." She grabbed her clothes, hurrying to get dressed. Her phone pinged again. More messages from Tim.

The final day of the festival had arrived and as they'd feared, the storm making a slow trek through the mountains left them with several feet of snow over night and the imminent threat of an avalanche. Add to that the notification that had gone out from Tim that a skier was missing and everyone would be on high alert.

"I'll come with ye," Bear said.

"We could probably use the help. A lot of the search and rescue people haven't been able to check in at the mountain. The roads are impassable and the ones who live out of town can't get through. Tim actually asked me to gather as many people as I could."

Bear was out of bed and at her side in a flash. They dressed and were through the door in no time. "We should stop at the ranch," he said. "Kade, Payton and Ross will want to join us."

"I'll call Ross and have them meet us at the search and rescue headquarters. We don't have time to stop."

The road from her house to the mountain had been plowed, but the snow was piling up again. It would be a constant battle to keep the road clear. Luckily she had chains on her car. She drove as fast as was safe in these conditions and finally arrived at headquarters and then went in search of Tim. "I'll be right back. Tim's probably in his office."

Bear waited at the large windows that looked out over the ski slopes, eyes straining for any evidence of the missing skier.

"Here, put this on," Kirsten said, handing Bear something unfamiliar.

"What is it?"

"It's a transceiver. Everyone will be wearing one just in case there's an avalanche. We normally would set one off before anyone went out on the mountain, but we've got a missing skier and we don't want to accidentally bury them. Here. Let me." She took the transceiver from his hand and after explaining how it worked, attached it inside his coat.

"Is anyone else coming?" Tim asked as he came out of his office.

"Ross will be here with Kade and Payton. He's spreading the word around town, so we should see help here soon. I can't believe it's just you and me."

"The snow has kept the rest of our crew from making it in. They'll keep trying, but for now we'll have to coordinate the search." He turned to Bear, his hand outstretched. "Thank you for helping. I know we've had our differences, but I'm grateful you're here."

Without saying a word, Bear nodded and shook Tim's hand.

Tim pulled a radio out from a box behind his desk. "You'll need this, too. I've already checked all the radios and they're good to go."

"Fresh batteries?" Kirsten asked.

"Yes."

The door opened and Ross, Kade and Payton came in. Kirsten set them all up with transceivers and radios. "We're going to have to split up for our search."

"I've flagged each section on the map. Kirsten you take Hills One and Two. Bear, you'll be over here on Hill Six." The rest of you will be on Hills Three through Five. I'm going to stay here so that when more people show up I can direct them. Kirsten will show you what to do." He picked up binoculars from his desk and headed to the windows.

"Come with me," Kirsten said, heading out the door and towards the chair lifts. "The mountain is closed today, but we've got the lifts running so we can get to the top and start our search from there." She gave them directions to follow in the event of an avalanche and repeated herself, making sure they all knew that first and foremost they wouldn't be able to outrun one, so it was best to move to the side if possible, to grab onto a tree or rock or something that might keep them from being dragged down with the cascade of snow and if they did find themselves buried not to panic but to try to create breathing room around them. The transceiver would help the others find them.

Once she was sure they all knew what to do, she escorted them to the lifts that would take each of them to the top of their particular slope and search area.

Bear was the last to go up and Kirsten had a sinking feeling in the pit of her stomach as she gave him final instructions. "Be careful. I don't want to lose you."

He gazed into her eyes, all seriousness. "Ye will no'." He lifted her chin and kissed her. "I'll call to ye if I find them."

She watched him as the ski lift took him up and then hurried to her own search area.

Bear rode the ski lift to the very top of the mountain, slipping off and moving to a spot where he could survey the terrain. He briefly wondered if he or his brothers were caught in an avalanche whether it would carry them back to their own time. No one here seemed to think that was possible, but it could be. Bear, Kade and Payton had proven that on the day they arrived in this time.

He took his time descending the slope towards the treeline. He felt sure that if the skier were lost on his slope the best places to find them would be in the trees. The unbroken white slope in front of him told him he was right. He moved further down the slope, slowly getting closer to the trees. A loud boom behind him stopped him in his tracks and as he looked back up the slope he saw a wall of snow heading towards him. He did as Kirsten had told him, moving to the side and towards the trees. The snow was on him before he had a chance to get very far and he did his best to stay on top of the sliding mass as it dragged him further downhill, eventually burying him. He had remembered to keep one arm straight up and created a small breathing pocket. His legs were pinned and he couldn't get purchase to push himself out of the snow. He had to trust the transceiver thing Kirsten gave him would work. There was nothing left to do but wait.

Kirsten heard the sound of an artillery blast on Hill Six where Bear was searching and her heart jumped into her throat. What was going on? They weren't supposed to set off an avalanche until they found their missing skier. She grabbed her radio.

"Bear," she called into it.

"What was that?" Ross's voice came through to her.

"Someone set off an avalanche on Bear's slope. We need to get over there now." She hurried as quickly as she could, skiing to the bottom of slope one and then across to the place where she'd left Bear only a short time ago. The others would be coming down the lifts, but she wasn't going to wait there for them. She had to get to Bear. If he was buried, there wouldn't be much time to save him. Taking the lift to the top, she called out his name over and over again, then tried reaching him on the radio. She waited for a reply, but none came. When she reached the top, she checked for his transceiver and it was pinging. That was a relief. She'd be able to find him, but she had to hurry. She found the spot where the snow had fractured and followed the transceiver to a spot close to the trees. She unstrapped the shovel from her back and began to dig. Panic had seized her, making her unsure of herself. Was she in the right spot? Should she try somewhere else. Ross and the others passed overhead on the ski lift. She waved up at them to make sure they'd seen her.

What if she couldn't find him? Would that mean that he'd gone back to his own time? It only heightened her anxiety. She had to find him. He had to be alright and he had to still be here.

She continued shoveling, concentrating on the transceiver. She knew she was in the right spot. She'd practiced this so many times and she knew how to do this. A disturbing thought came to mind as she remembered that Tim had stayed behind. He'd picked where Bear would be and while she'd been surprised that he'd put him all the way on the other side of the mountain, she didn't think too much about it. Had Tim been trying to kill Bear? Did he try to run Bear over with the snowmobile the other night? Or shoot at him yesterday? Was he even capable of this?

The next shovelful revealed a hand sticking straight up in the snow. "Yes!" She'd found him. "I'm here, Bear. Stay with me. You're going to be okay."

Ross and the brothers were at her side. "Help me. We've got to get him out of there. By her calculation, he'd been under for almost thirty minutes. If he didn't have an air pocket her efforts would be useless, but if he did, they only had seconds to get him out. All four of them began shoveling snow out of the way and before long, they found him, eyes closed and very still. Ross and Kade grabbed him under his arms and pulled him out, but he was limp, and not moving.

"Lay him down," Kirsten ordered. "Ross, do you know CPR?"

"I do. Cassie trained me."

"Good. Let's get to work." Cassie cleared his airways of any snow and began mouth-to-mouth. Tears streamed down her cheeks as she continued. She and Ross worked as a team. It was taking too long, but she wasn't going to give up. She couldn't. She loved this man and she'd only just found him. She wasn't about to lose him.

Bear's eyes opened as he gasped for breath.

"You're alive," Kirsten exclaimed, throwing herself on top of him.

"What happened?" he asked.

"You were caught in an avalanche."

"And I'm still here." A crooked grin appeared on his face.

She was crying uncontrollably now. Relief and the knowledge that he'd almost died overwhelming her.

"Are ye no' happy about that?" he asked.

She wiped her face on her sleeve. "More than you know." It was all she could manage to get out. Her breath seemed to be caught in her throat as she reached out a hand to touch his cheek. He grabbed it and put it to his lips.

"Thank ye for saving me."

"We've got to get you back down the mountain and warm you up."

Kade lifted him from behind while Ross and Payton each positioned themselves on either side of him. He placed an arm around each of their necks.

"Did you break anything?" Kirsten asked.

"I'm too cold to feel anything," Bear replied.

The men set off towards the chairlifts and Kirsten took a moment to get on the radio. "Tim, over."

"I'm here, over."

"What the hell was that all about?"

There was a long pause on the other end of the radio. "I don't know what you mean."

"I heard the blast on Hill Six. Who ordered it?"

No reply came through. She was steaming mad. Someone set that blast off and she was going to find out who and why. Once they had Bear to safety, they'd continue the search for the lost skier. But

Kirsten had a sneaking suspicion there was no skier and this had all been a ruse to get Bear out on the mountain alone.

Once at the bottom of the hill, they got Bear into the lodge. It was empty except for the staff managing the information desk and the kitchen crew.

"What happened?" the girl behind the desk asked.

"Someone set off an avalanche. He's lucky to be alive."

"I'll call for an EMT," she offered.

"Thanks."

They sat Bear near the fire, helping to remove his jacket. One of the kitchen crew came out with a blanket and wrapped it around his shoulders. Bear seemed comfortable enough that Kirsten wasn't too concerned about broken bones. He seemed to be in pretty good condition considering what he'd just been through.

"Ross, can I talk to you for a minute?" Kirsten took hold of his elbow and guided him away from the brothers.

"I'm not sure, but I think Tim may have purposely set off that avalanche. It wasn't an accident."

"Are ye sure?"

"He was in the office keeping watch. He would've been the only one there who could have ordered it." She turned to the information desk. "Have you heard anything about a missing skier?" Kirsten knew that if anyone was unaccounted for, all of the staff would be aware of it.

"No. We haven't heard a thing."

"How did you get here today?"

"The usual route."

"Wasn't it closed?"

"No. It was cleared bright and early this morning."

Kirsten turned back to Ross. "He lied. I don't think there's a missing skier and the search and rescue crew could definitely have made it here despite the snow."

"I'm going to go back to headquarters and confront him."

"I dinnae believe that to be wise," Ross said.

"I'll be fine." She turned to the girl at the information counter. "Call the sheriff and ask him to meet me at search and rescue headquarters."

"Will do."

"Take care of Bear. The EMTs should be here soon."

Kirsten sprinted out the door and headed straight for search and rescue. She was livid, but in order to do this, she was going to have to calm down first. She took several deep breaths as she walked, talking herself down from the heightened state of anger she was in.

The snow was still falling heavily, but she noted several more vehicles parked outside of headquarters.

"Hey, Kirsten," one of her co-workers greeted her holding the doors open so she could pass through. "You look like a woman on a mission."

"I am. Where's Tim?"

"He took off out of here about ten minutes ago. He was in quite a hurry for some reason."

"Do any of you know anything about a missing skier?"

"No. We weren't notified of anything when we spoke with Tim earlier."

"You spoke with Tim this morning?"

"Yeah. He called us all to tell us he didn't need us here until later."

That pretty much told Kirsten all she needed to know. She headed back outside to wait for the sheriff as he pulled up in front of the building.

"What's going on?" he asked.

Kirsten filled him in on what had happened and told him Tim was the one who had orchestrated the whole thing. "I knew he was jealous of Bear, but I never thought he was capable of trying to kill him."

"I'm going to put a call out to the highway patrol to be on the lookout for him. In the meantime, I'm going to speak with everyone here. I'll see if any of them know anything."

✳

The waiting room at the hospital was filled with well wishers. Once word got out about what had happened, they all congregated together to lend their support.

"Bear refused to go to the hospital, so we had to force the issue." Cassie explained to everyone. "He seems fine though."

"The doctor says another small group can join us in his room," Kirsten said as she entered the waiting room.

Rose, Walt, Cassie, Amy and Sue all stood and followed Kirsten down the corridor to Bear's room, where they joined the others already there. No one seemed ready to leave. "We'll see how long the nurses let us all stay," Kirsten said.

"Oh, my gosh, Bear, are you okay?" Amy said, grabbing hold of his hand.

"I'm fine," Bear announced as he struggled to sit up.

Kirsten used the bed control to raise him up to a sitting position.

Everyone applauded once he was upright, much to his delight.

"We're so happy you're okay," Cassie said, hurrying to his side and gingerly hugging him.

"No more so than I," Bear smiled. He was flanked by Kirsten, his brothers and Ross.

"So, Tim?" Sue asked.

"Yes. There seems to be plenty of evidence to suggest he was trying to kill Bear out of jealousy," Cassie said.

"Wow! I can hardly believe it." Rose said. "He seemed like such a nice young man."

"Kirsten," Bear held out his hand to her. "Come sit with me."

"You're still here," she said, a wide smile spreading across her face. She sat on the edge of the bed, stroking his hand.

"And I'm staying." He smiled brightly at this. The decision had been made for him by the fates and he couldn't be happier. The

189

thought of never seeing Kirsten again had jolted him as he lay in his cold, snowy grave. He thought he was going to die and his only thoughts were of her.

Ross's phone rang and he picked it up. "Yes." He was quiet as he listened to whoever was on the other end of the phone. "Thank you."

"That was the sheriff. It seems Tim's car drove off the side of the road as he was trying to get away. He was killed."

There were several gasps heard around the room.

"People who were driving on the road at the time heard an earsplitting howl and saw a tall, grey man on the side of the road right where Tim's car veered down the embankment."

Kade's head popped up, his eyes wide. *"Am Fear Liath Mor.* He's here. He was angry that Tim tried to kill Bear."

"The Old Grey Man," Ross said, shaking his head.

"I thought he was just a legend," Cassie said.

"He's your protector, Bear," Kirsten said.

His mind was reeling. The Old Grey Man sent him here to this time and place. To this woman. Why he had sent Tim to his grave was more than he wanted to think about at this moment. It was enough to know that Bear was meant to be here. It was as if he'd been given a second chance. A new life awaited him and he was ready for it.

CHAPTER 18

"**W**ell, the festival was a huge success," Cassie announced to the group gathered for brunch at her dining room table.

Excited chatter filled the room as everyone agreed with her announcement. They'd postponed the brunch until Bear was out of the hospital and could join them. He'd stayed the night for observation, but felt well enough when he was released to head straight to the ranch with Kirsten. Everyone responsible for the festival was in attendance as they celebrated their good fortune. They were also celebrating the fact that Bear didn't seem any worse for wear after his brush with death on the slopes. Rose presented him with a beautiful cake she'd decorated especially for him. She somehow managed to create a replica of the Fletcher tartan and their family crest.

"'Tis beautiful." Bear held the cake in his hands, awestruck by what he was seeing. "How did ye do it?"

"Trade secret," Rose teased. "But your brother helped."

"Kade, no, ye did no'." Bear couldn't believe it. He was touched by all the love he felt from all the good people in this room.

"Rose is a good teacher," Kade said, beaming at Rose and wrapping an arm around her shoulders.

"Well, thank ye both," Bear said.

A knock at the door quieted them momentarily while Cassie went to see who it was. Kirsten squeezed Bear's hand under the table and leaned her head on his shoulder. The shock of everything that had happened the day before was wearing off, but she wasn't ready to leave his side. He returned the squeeze and leaned over to kiss her cheek.

"Sheriff Stengahl, please come in." Cassie said.

"I've got news about Tim," he replied.

"Of course. Let me get Kirsten and Bear."

"No need. We're here," Kirsten said, approaching the sheriff. Ross and the brothers joined them.

"I wanted to let you all know that we did a thorough search of Tim's apartment and we found a journal that he'd been keeping. I won't go into the details, but I will say that he was obsessed with you, Kirsten."

"He also left detailed plans to get rid of Bear. He was jealous and wanted you dead. All of the strange things that were happening, including the break in at your home, were orchestrated by him."

"I never would have thought it in a million years," Kirsten said. Her stomach churned as the full weight of what Sheriff Stengahl was saying settled in. "I know he was having a hard time letting go of me, but I never believed he was capable of killing someone."

"I've got more work to do before I can put this case to bed. I'll probably need to talk to the two of you some time today if you don't mind," he said to Kirsten and Bear.

"Of course. The sooner this is over with the better," Kirsten replied. She leaned heavily on Bear for support. "This is all my fault. If only I'd noticed sooner."

"That's ridiculous," Cassie said. "This was in no way your fault. It was all Tim's doing. He was the sick one. You are not responsible for his actions."

"I'll be at the station. Come by and see me later," Sheriff Stengahl said. Cassie showed him to the door before escorting everyone back to the dining room.

"Let's all finish our brunch. We can enjoy a brief respite before we start planning our next event." Cassie poured coffee into any empty cups she came across and then joined everyone else at the table.

The chatter started up again as everyone spoke with those sitting closest to them. Kirsten glanced at Bear whose eyes were intently focused on her.

"Are ye alright, lass?" he asked.

"As long as you're here by my side the answer is always going to be yes."

Bear stood outside in the cold with his brothers. Somehow they'd gotten lucky. Kade was healthy and fit once again. Payton was able to keep busy here at the ranch. Back home he'd been miserable. Everything there was a terrible reminder of all he'd lost. As for Bear, he felt he was the luckiest. He had Kirsten. He wasn't sure what normal looked like here in Delight, but he hoped to find out. Since their arrival they'd been engulfed in preparations for the festival and then the festival itself. Now, a few days had passed since it had ended and he was excited to see where this life would lead him and his brothers. It would be good to see what life was like here when it wasn't so busy. He imagined many lazy days and nights spent with Kirsten in his arms. He was ready for that. Ready to settle down, start a family and work. Kirsten had assured him that he would have many opportunities to be useful here in Delight.

"Just look at Ross," she'd told him. "Maybe we can get you certified so that you can work with the ski patrol, but in the meantime I'll need you at the shop."

It all sounded wonderful to him. He really didn't think he'd mind do anything at all here in Delight. Kade seemed to have found a job at the bakery. Rose was pleased with his work and told him she'd teach him to bake more than just cookies.

Yes, Bear was happy. Perhaps happier than he'd ever been in his life and he was glad to share it with Kade and Payton. He loved his brothers more than he could express, but he was sure they knew it. Glancing at them now, he dreaded telling them that he would no longer be sharing the cabin with them, but they'd know soon enough, so he'd better get it over with. "I'll be staying with Kirsten from now on," he told them.

"We gathered as much. We'll miss ye brother," Kade said.

"Ye'll still see me. I'll be here often for Cassie's fine cooking." He glanced from Kade to Payton. "If ye need me at any time of day or night…"

"We ken it," Payton said.

Bear felt guilty. He'd found love while his brother was grieving the loss of his. "I'm sorry, Payton."

"Bear do no' be sorry. Ye deserve love. All these years ye've been caring for us and our clan. Now 'tis time for ye to have what ye have always wanted. Do no' fash for me. I will heal."

"What of ye, Kade?" Bear asked.

"I'm happier than I've ever been," he said. "I feared we'd have to go back. I was no' sure how I would get the toaster, the coffee maker and all my new clothes into a pack to take with me. I be happy to stay and even happier that my two brothers will be here with me."

The three men formed a circle, hugging each other for all they were worth. Bear didn't want to let go, but he knew that in this time they would be safe and he could leave some of his brotherly duties. He would still, of course, take care of them, but he no longer felt responsible for them. They were grown men and it was time for him to let go.

"Looks like you're going to have a new roommate." Amy was full of energy this morning. It was one of the things Kirsten admired about her. It had been a week since their celebratory brunch at the end of the festival. Cassie had invited everyone back because she wasn't quite ready to let go of the festival excitement. Amy was helping Cassie clean up now that everyone was done eating. She did the dishes, put the food away and made sure the counters were as clean as a whistle. Ross and the brothers had gone out to do some work around the ranch. Bear was in the barn with his other girl, Evie.

Kirsten sat back on the sofa admiring her two best friends. "I'm excited to have Bear living with me."

"I'll bet he's pretty excited, too." Cassie said, sitting beside Kirsten.

"That's an understatement," Kirsten said.

"We'll miss you." A fake pout sprouted on Amy's lips.

"I'm not going anywhere," Kirsten protested.

"At least be sure to come out of that house of yours every now and again," Cassie teased.

"I have to work," Kirsten smiled. "I can't spend all my time locked up with Bear. Although that does sound kind of nice right now."

"You've given me hope." Amy's sweet face grew serious. Her sincerity shining through.

"What do you mean?" Kirsten asked.

"I never thought it would be possible for any of us to find love here in Delight, but you've both proven me wrong."

Kirsten tipped her head onto Amy's shoulder and Cassie did the same on the other side.

"I didn't even realize how alone I felt. I know I had both of you and Sue in my life, but it's not the same." Kirsten felt truly blessed. She'd not only found the man of her dreams, but she had the best friends a girl could ever want.

"I know what you mean," Cassie said. "I felt the same way with Ross. I was sure I was going to turn in to a cranky old lady all alone in that big cabin on the hill. It all changed faster than I could have imagined. It will for you, too, Amy."

"I hope so. Otto's great company, but even he would love it if I found a guy he could play ball with.

"I have no doubt you will," Kirsten said. "I'm excited to see what this next chapter of my life will bring. One thing is for sure, no more lonely nights eating dinner alone."

"You had Kirby," Amy teased.

"True. And you have Otto."

"He's my rock." Amy laughed. She took hold of Kirsten's hand and then Cassie's. "Only good things from now on for all of us."

"Amen to that," Kirsten answered.

Following the sounds of whistling and rustling hay, Kirsten found Bear in the barn with Evie.

"Hey, you," she greeted him.

He handed her a brush so she could help groom the mare. "I feel a weight has been lifted from me," he said.

"I know what you mean." Or at least she thought she might. She hadn't been aware of all the hardships he and his brothers had endured and when she found out it only drew her closer to him. He was a good man. One you could count on no matter the situation.

Bear was silent for a while, concentrating on Evie who was enjoying his attention a great deal.

Kirsten was content to wait for him to speak. She knew he would when he was ready.

He glanced across Evie's rump, smiling at her. "Ye ken I was torn between wanting to stay here with ye and my responsibility to my clan. Now I ken I was never meant to return to them. This is where I belong. Here with ye."

"You knew it all along, didn't you?"

"I did. Deep inside I always knew."

Bear ran a comb through Evie's tail.

"She's beautiful," Kirsten said.

"She is, but not near as beautiful as ye, my love."

What could she say to that? This man who'd appeared out of nowhere had become the most important thing in her life. He was all she'd ever dreamed she wanted in a man. There wasn't a false bone in his body. He said what he meant and she knew that if he loved you, he would always be there for you. She stopped brushing and went to his side.

"I love you Bear Fletcher."

"I love ye, Kirsten Hunter." He wrapped her in his arms, kissing her with a love and passion she returned. This was only the beginning of their story. They had a lifetime to write the rest of it together.

EPILOGUE

"Ye promised me we'd spend the next few weeks in bed. Are ye telling me ye've changed yer mind?" Bear asked, his bare chest peeking up from the now tangled sheets.

"I didn't think you really believed me. I can't spend two weeks in bed, as much as I'd love to." Kirsten touched the tip of his nose with her finger. Two weeks in bed with Bear would hardly be enough.

"Alright. One week then." He propped himself on his elbow, taking her chin in his hand.

Kirsten rolled her eyes in her head. "Are you negotiating with me?"

"I am."

"I can give you this weekend, but after that I have to get back to work. I'm the new safety team leader here in Delight." She was proud of herself for asking for the job and even prouder that she'd received it.

"Hmmm... one weekend. I'll take it." Bear grabbed Kirsten around the waist, pulling her down to the bed.

Kirby looked particularly put out when he had to move to make room for her. "I think that cat loves you more than me, the woman who's been feeding him all these years."

"Ye could be right," Bear said as Kirby climbed back on the bed and head butted him. "But ye ken who I love more than Kirby and I do no' even care if she feeds me?"

"Who?"

"Ye." He pulled her close and softly kissed her lips. "Ye are a blessing to me. And I believe ye are the reason the Grey Man sent me here."

"I'll have to thank him if I ever see him." Kirsten wasn't sure she believed the whole Grey Man theory.

Bear chuckled. "As grateful as I be to him, I hope to never see him or hear him again."

"Scared, huh?" she teased.

Bear crossed his arms over his perfectly muscled chest causing Kirsten's eyes to go wide. "I'm no' scared. He likes me."

"Like the cat."

"Yer a funny one, lass. I think I'll keep ye."

"If anyone's doing the keeping around here, it's me." She was onto him and knew exactly what he was up to. A bit more playful banter and muscle flexing and he'd have her right where he wanted her, but much to her surprise, his face became serious as he took her hand in his.

"I love ye, Kirsten. I'm hoping ye'll agree to be me wife."

"I love you, too." She couldn't have been more surprised. "And are you asking me to marry you?"

"I believe I am. What say ye?"

"Yes. Yes. I'll be your wife." She shrieked with joy as she leaped from the bed.

"Why do ye run? Do ye wish to get away from me?"

"I'm not running. I'm excited to be your wife." She jumped back on the bed, rolling on top of him. Kirby looked disgusted as he hopped off the bed and left the room.

"Alone at last, me love." Bear took her face in his hands, kissing her. "I'm a happy man."

"I'm a happy woman." *And I'm right where I want to be.*

ACKNOWLEDGMENTS

I am forever grateful to my editor, Jen Graybeal, for her suggestions, corrections and help polishing Wanted. I am also thankful for my cover artist, Sheri McGathy. Sheri always knows exactly what I want and goes above and beyond to create it for me. Thank you to my husband, who understands that when I'm writing I sometimes forget what time it is and that means he has to make his own supper. And last, but not least, thank you to all my fur babies for always being by my side.

ABOUT THE AUTHOR

Jennae Vale is a best selling author of romance with a touch of magic. As a history buff from an early age, Jennae often found herself daydreaming in history class and wondering what it would be like to live in the places and time periods she was learning about. Writing time travel romance has given her an opportunity to take those daydreams and turn them into stories to share with readers everywhere.

Originally from the Boston area, Jennae now lives in the San Francisco Bay area, where some of her characters also reside. When Jennae isn't writing, she enjoys spending time with her family and her pets, and daydreaming, of course.

ALSO BY JENNAE VALE

THE THISTLE & HIVE SERIES

A Bridge Through Time

A Thistle Beyond Time

Separated By Time

A Matter of Time

A Thistle & Hive Christmas

A Turn In Time

All In Good Time

A Long Forgotten Time

Awakened By Time

Saved By Time

THE MACKALLS OF DUNNET HEAD

Her Trusted Highlander

Her Noble Highlander

Her Mysterious Highlander

OTHER BOOKS BY THIS AUTHOR

A Highlander In Vegas

Ross

A NOTE FROM JENNAE

Thank you so much for reading Wanted: Delight Book One. If you enjoyed the book and have a minute to spare, I would really appreciate a short review on the page or site where you bought the book. Your help in spreading the word is greatly appreciated. Reviews from readers like you make a huge difference in helping new readers find stories similar to Wanted.

If you'd like to know when my next book comes out and want to receive occasional updates from me, then you can sign up for my newsletter here http://eepurl.com/bf1CqP

CPSIA information can be obtained
at www.ICGtesting.com
Printed in the USA
BVHW040918170319
542892BV00016B/241/P